MAE'S REVENGE

By: L. C. Bennett Stern

Mae's Revenge
by L.C. Bennett Stern
Copyright 2017 by L.C. Bennett Stern

All rights reserved. No part of this publication may be reproduced, stored in a retrieval system, transmitted in any form or by any means, electronic, mechanical, photocopying, recording, or otherwise, without prior written permission of the publisher and author except for brief quotations in reviews and articles.

ISBN: 978-1547078745
Printed in United States of America
Cover design and text layout by Parry Design Studio, Inc. (www.parrydesign.com)

Also by L.C. Bennett Stern:

Bosses and Blackjacks:
A Tale of the "Bloody Fifth" in Philadelphia

(Available: Amazon, Barnesandnoble.com, and
Pipe & Thimble Bookstore, Lomita, CA)

Award-Winning Finalist in the
"True Crime: Non-Fiction" category of the
2017 International Book Awards

"A fascinating tale of politics in Philadelphia in the early 1900s. The courtroom scenes were well-written and the book captured the political corruption at the time. A recommended read."

"It seemed like we were right there living each day with Officer Bennett and his family, along with the everyday financial and emotional struggles they faced. At one point in the book I found myself grieving for the loss of a family member and other parts were so realistic that it brought chills to me. I would definitely recommend this book."

"I loved this book. Had a hard time putting it down at night. I grew up in the Midwest and I guess very naive about such things really happening."

"Incredible true story crafted into a highly enjoyable novel. The author's dedication to research makes early-20th century Philadelphia come alive again!"

—Amazon Reviews

Dedicated to all the women throughout history
who have persevered, in order to realize their dreams.

And always

to Michael, Amanda, and Joshua

"Close by were the 'hurdy-gurdies,' where the music from asthmatic pianos timed the dancing of painted, padded and leering Aspasias, too hideous to hope for a livelihood in any village less remote from civilization."

—*Black Hills Daily Pioneer* of September 23, 1876

PART ONE

The Gem Variety Theater and Dance Hall

Al Swearengen recruited women from the east by advertising jobs in hotels and promising to make them stage performers at his theater. Purchasing a one-way ticket for the women, when they arrived, the hapless ladies would find themselves stranded with little choice other than to work for the notorious Swearengen or be thrown into the street. Some of these desperate women took their own lives rather than being forced into a position of virtual slavery. Those who stayed were known to sport constant bruises and other injuries.

—Kathy Weiser, owner/editor;
legendsofamerica.com

CHAPTER ONE

"**But Mama,** you know I've always dreamed of being an actress. This is my big chance!"

"Don't talk nonsense, Mae. You've never even been on a train. What makes you think you, a seventeen-year-old girl, would be safe traveling way out to South Dakota all alone? Besides, we don't have money for such a trip."

"I won't need any money, and I'm almost eighteen. It says right here in the newspaper that all expenses will be paid by Mr. Swearengen, proprietor of the Gem Theater."

"Mae, you know your Papa will not hear of it. We need you here in the shop. Papa says 1888 will be our busiest year yet since coming to Philadelphia. He has so many orders for men's waistcoats, he's thinking of ordering another Singer treadle machine."

Nathan Steinberg walked through the frayed, black-curtained doorway into the back room of his tailor shop,

Mae's Revenge

where his wife and daughter had their heads together, whispering, as if planning some sort of rebellion.

"So? Vot's so important you haven't yet finished with those buttonholes? Hmm? Which one of you will tell the Papa?"

"Sorry, Papa."

Mae put her head down and concentrated on her sewing.

"Sorry, Papa? That's the answer I get? Vot have you two been cooking up back here? And don't try to tell me nothing. I know when the women get their heads close, this means something."

His wife let out a big sigh, and then blurted, "Mae wants to go be an actress in South Dakota. So there! Now you know."

Mae stole a quick glance at her father's face, which was turning crimson.

"Ha! You make a joke. A Steinberg … an actress … in South Dakota. That is a very funny joke. Now, tell me vot is really going on back here, Fanny."

"It's true. That is what we were talking. Mae saw this in the newspaper today."

Fanny handed her husband the paper and quickly turned away as he read. She did not want to watch the familiar beard-stroking frown overtake the gentle face she loved so much.

Mae tried to disappear into her seat by bending over as far as she could into the sewing on her lap. *What was I thinking? An actress? Me?* She wanted to jump up and grab the newspaper from her father's hands and run out into the street and get run down by the trolley—and then everyone would feel sorry for her and pet her and tell her she could be anything she wanted, and her father would forget why he was so angry with her and he would buy her flowers.

That is not what happened.

Once he finished reading, Nathan Steinberg placed the newspaper on the little table perched between his wife and daughter and walked back through the curtained doorway without saying a word.

Mae looked after him and then to her mother. "What is he doing, Mama? Why didn't he say something?"

"I have no idea. Better we should not talk about this anymore. Hand me that black thread."

"But Mama—we have to talk about it." She passed the spool of thread. "I *am* going. He has to know."

"Listen to your Mama. Give him a little time to think on this. Wait until he talks of it. That will be best." Fanny threaded the needle with black and said, "Ja, that will be best."

Mae looked pleadingly at her mother. She felt her mouth open to speak, but there were no words, and she winced as the needle pricked and her finger began to bleed.

She reached into the pocket of her apron for a handkerchief to staunch the flow and scraped the palm of her hand on the edge of the train ticket to South Dakota. *How will I ever convince them by Thursday? That gives me only three days, and I've got so much to do before then.*

Mae stopped the bleeding and rubbed her red-rimmed eyes. For the past two weeks, she had been sneaking back down into the shop while everyone else slept, and now it was taking its toll. The traveling outfits she made herself were close to being complete. Tonight should do it. The buttons on the blue shirtwaist should take her no time at all. Then she could pack it in with the other garments wrapped in brown paper and tucked behind the bolts of gabardine in the corner of the stuffy workroom.

"Mae, stop with the daydreaming," her mother interrupted. "There's much work to be done."

Her mother always knew when her mind had drifted away. Mae didn't know how she knew, but she did. *I'm going to miss her most.* Mae sighed and went back to the buttonholes with clouds in her eyes.

That night at supper, upstairs in their cramped apartment, Mae couldn't wait until the meal was finished, when her Papa would light his pipe and talking was allowed.

Mae was certain spending the rest of her life in this tight-knit Philadelphia neighborhood where everyone knew your business would eventually force her to do something desperate. As she buttered another biscuit, she envisioned herself perched on the edge of the rooftop. The crowd of spectators below gnashing their teeth, begging her not to jump. The pleading looks of her parents. "Why didn't we let her go out West to become an actress? She would have been happy there." But now it was too late! She edged closer to the precipice and looked down on their pitiful upturned faces …

"Mae. Mae! Pass your father the potatoes."

"Sorry, Mama."

Will this meal never end?

Her two younger brothers shoveled food into their mouths like the hogs she knew they would grow up to be. Mae had to look down at her own plate to avoid watching their wretched gobbling. For a moment she actually thought she heard them snort as they ate. *Disgusting. I can't wait to get away from them.*

"Papa, are you ready for your pipe? I'll be happy to get it for you."

"Mae, do you see me still eating? No talking. When I'm ready for my pipe, I will say so."

Mae looked to her mother, but got no indication help would be coming soon, so she slumped back in her chair and folded her arms. To wait. And wait.

At last, he put down his fork, wiped his mouth with the back of his hand, and looked over at his agitated daughter. "Now, Mae, you can get me my pipe."

"Certainly, Papa." She was sure he was going to discuss with her what he had read in the newspaper that afternoon.

"So. Tell me, boys, did you give to Mama your pay for sweeping up at Mr. Goldstein's today?"

Mae could not believe her ears. She'd been waiting for hours to discuss a major life-changing decision with her Papa, and what did he care about? The five cents her brothers earned for dragging a broom across their neighbor's floor. His lack of consideration for her feelings hardened her resolve to leave. *Thursday cannot come fast enough. I'll get on that train and I won't even wave good-bye. He'll cry himself to sleep worrying about me. Out there in the world. All alone. His little girl. No one to look after her. No one to fetch his pipe.*

"Now, tell me, Mae. What is this craziness of yours? To be an actress in South Dakota?"

He won't sleep for weeks. He'll become sick with worry. Mama will call the doctor to come ....

Mae's Revenge

"Mae! Your father is talking to you!" Her mother always knew.

"Wh—what?"

"Tell me of this trip you have planned without talking first to your Papa."

Her brothers cut in to ask if they could go outside to play with the other boys in the neighborhood.

"Shoo. Shoo. Go—but only on the block," their mother told them. "And put on your jackets—it's still cold outside and you don't want to get the croup."

"They're always interrupting!" Mae said. "I can't wait to get away and be around human beings who know how to behave!"

Nathan stopped mid-draw on his pipe. "They're just boys, Mae. Now tell me of this plan of yours."

"Yes, Papa." Mae stood and began pacing as she regaled her father with her tale of wanderlust—waving her arms in the air and crossing her hands over her heart for dramatic effect as she spoke. She flopped down onto her chair, both arms weakly dangling by her sides, as she finished her prepared speech with tears streaming down her freckled cheeks. "So you can see why I simply must go, can't you Papa?"

Nathan stared at his daughter, but said nothing.

"And Mama said it is alright, if you say it is alright."

Her mother's eyes darted in her direction, but she stayed quiet.

Nathan looked to his wife and then back at his daughter's hopeful expression.

"Vell, if this performance is any show of what an actress you will make, then I say …"

Mae held her breath.

"Ja! You can go."

"Oh, Papa! Thank you, Papa!" Mae jumped up and covered his head with kisses.

Pushing her away, Nathan added, "But if you do this thing, you must know you are on your own. Your Mama and your Papa will not be there to protect you, to feed you, and keep you warm. This will be only for you to do, all alone. We do not have money to come rescue you. Do you understand?"

"Yes, Papa. I understand. I'll be fine. You'll see."

That evening, Mae passed her two rowdy brothers scampering up the steps, mocking her in sing-song, "Mae's an old maid! Mae's an old maid!" as she walked down to the shop to finish sewing her traveling clothes. Now that she no longer had to hide what she was doing, Mae didn't have to wait until everyone went to bed. She began humming "A Hot Time in the Old Town" as she poked the thread through the eye of the needle.

CHAPTER TWO

Thursday morning arrived with a thunderclap! Mae couldn't believe it. *Not another April storm. Not today of all days. Papa will not want me walking through thunder and lightning to get the train. Why must I suffer endlessly? Will my existence ever be happy and carefree?*

Her patchwork quilt came alive with flashes dancing across her small cot by the window. She looked over at her two annoying little brothers sleeping blissfully, unaware of the monsoon outside. *How can they sleep through this? They must be dead. No, I take that back. I didn't mean it.* She knocked on the wooden windowsill to erase the mean thoughts she had about them. After all, today was the last day, for who knew how long, she would have to deal with them. *I know they're going to miss me and cry when I leave. I might even write to them occasionally.*

Nathan Steinberg handed the valise to his daughter and also handed her an envelope. Mae looked up at him quizzically. "Did you think I would send you, my little flower, to South Dakota without a penny? Sorry we have not enough money to put you on a Pullman car so you could sleep safely some of the way." He brushed away the tears threatening his cheeks with the backs of his hands and then hugged her close one last time. "Now, go, go. Get out of the rain. The train will leave without you!"

The platform overflowed with men, women, and children juggling luggage and bundles holding food for the trip, while hugging and kissing their good-byes. The train's whistle began to blow.

Mae tried to give her Papa a reassuring smile. She managed no more than a tight grin. "I'll write to you as soon as I'm settled—I promise!" Thunder clapped. She began to back away toward the open door of the train car, but rushed back to him for one last embrace. Her parting kiss brushed his damp beard as she turned away to climb the steps. Her face shone with raindrops blended with cascading tears. The train began to pull out of the station as she settled into a seat by the window. She waved to her Papa until he became one of the tiny dots speckling the platform.

Mae was truly alone for the first time in her life. She didn't like the sensation of her throat tightening and the thumping in her chest. For a brief time, she thought she might be dying, but within moments, a well-dressed, meticulous older gentleman tipped his hat and asked if he might take the empty seat next to her. She glanced up into his pale blue eyes and immediately relaxed. Smiling, she said, "Certainly."

"Thank you, young lady. How do you do? My name is Reginald VanSant. And you are?"

"Mae. Uh, Annie Mae Steinberg, sir. Very pleased to meet you." She offered her hand.

"The pleasure is all mine, Miss Steinberg." VanSant took Mae's gloved hand and put it to his lips, all the while examining her bright green eyes.

Mae immediately withdrew her hand and folded it into her other one, placed them purposefully in her lap, and looked away.

"I didn't mean to offend you, Miss Steinberg, uh, may I call you Annie Mae?"

She wanted to give an air of confidence despite being frightened, and replied, "Makes no difference to me." She waved the air nonchalantly. "My friends all call me Mae."

"I would like us to be friends, Mae. After all, we have a long journey ahead of us and it will be much more pleasurable if we are friends, don't you think?"

What Mae was thinking was that she wished she were back at home, still in her bed by the window with her brothers snoring in their bed across the room. However, she responded, "Certainly, that would be better." As she spoke, she shifted closer to the window and added, "Oh my! Look! We're approaching the city limits!" It was hard to contain the excitement she felt, and her words came out a bit too loud.

VanSant chuckled. "Never away from home before?" he asked.

Mae wanted to maintain what she considered to be an adult demeanor and responded, "Of course I've been away before. I just never traveled west before. I've been east to New Jersey many times." In truth, she had only been as far east as the edge of the Delaware River on the Philadelphia side. She managed to see New Jersey from there and that vantage point proved good enough for her. She sniffed and detected a bit of alcohol on VanSant's breath, despite the early hour. She scooted ever closer to the window.

VanSant pulled a pipe from his inside pocket, opened a pouch of tobacco, pinched a bit between his fingers, and began tapping it into the bowl. "You don't mind if I have a smoke, do you, Mae?"

"Of course not, my father smokes a pipe every evening and I've grown accustomed to the aroma of a fine tobacco." *This man doesn't need to know I lived above a tailor's shop in a tiny apartment with four other people. I can tell him whatever story I want, and he has no way of knowing if I'm telling the truth or not!* This encouraged Mae to expand on her tale. "Why, when my family received the ambassador from Cuba, he presented my father with a sterling silver tin filled with the very finest tobacco the island had to offer."

"My, my! That is impressive, Mae," VanSant said and lit his pipe.

Mae breathed in the warm cherry tobacco scent and almost burst into tears. The sad expression on her father's face as she waved good-bye flashed past, but she subdued the image by imagining Mr. VanSant strolling by her side down Sixteenth Street back in the city. Mae saw he had no wrinkles to speak of. She guessed now, after having the chance to examine his face more closely, he was probably close to thirty years old. That's not that old, she told herself, as she felt, rather than saw, the countryside whizzing by. *All the neighbors would be rushing out onto their stoops or hanging out of second-story windows to get a glimpse of the magnificent pair, dressed in their finery. She, holding her silk parasol, with her lace-gloved hand resting on his forearm as he guided her smoothly along the brick walkway on a glorious Sunday afternoon.*

"Do you expect to continue on past Chicago, Mae?" VanSant quizzed her.

He would tell some humorous, intimate tale, and she would tilt her head into his broad shoulder in an embarrassed giggle.

"Mae, did you hear me?"

"I'm sorry, did you say something?" She felt the warm blush rising to her forehead.

"Yes. I asked if you expected to continue your trip beyond Chicago."

"Oh yes. Didn't I say? Yes. I'm going to South Dakota. You see, I'm to be an actress on the stage of the Gem Theater out there. That's why I'm on this train."

"An actress? How very exciting! I'm sure audiences will be thrilled to see you," VanSant told her.

Mae straightened her back and lifted her chin. "I'm sure, if you had an interest in attending one of my performances, arrangements for you to have a front-row seat might be arranged, Mr. VanSant."

"Please—call me Reginald."

"Very well. Reginald." *Papa would approve of such an obviously successful man. Certainly Reginald was a proper gentleman and would ask him for permission to marry her. Mama would be impressed with the size of the diamond engagement ring. I wonder where we will go on our honeymoon trip?*

VanSant tapped her arm. "Mae, we're pulling into the rest stop. Would you like to stretch your legs?"

Mae returned to reality with a start. "We're stopping? Why?" She saw the other passengers stand and stretch in the aisle before exiting the car. Mae looked through the soot-covered window to see where everyone was going. She saw several of the men traipsing into the woods to the left of the tracks. The ladies were queueing in front of a bank of outhouses to the right. It occurred to her that she should join them before the train got underway again.

"I'm afraid I won't have time for a stroll, judging by those lines, Reginald," she said, pointing in the direction of the female passengers. "Now, if you'll excuse me."

"Nature calls!" he said, and smiled.

Mae dropped her chin to her chest. *I must not blush. I must not blush.*

VanSant stood, held her arm at the elbow, and guided her off the train before making his way behind a dense outcropping of tall pines to relieve himself.

The curtain of ebony that came down on the day, obliterating the view outside the grimy window, and the feeling of the train gliding along the iron rails beneath her feet, with the monotonous bumpety-click, soothed Mae into a semiconscious stupor. The emotional exhaustion of leaving her family and trying to impress the man sitting next to her with witty conversation had taken its toll. Her head began to bob until Reginald caressed the side of her face and pulled her cheek onto his shoulder. Mae snuggled into a more comfortable position and drifted into a dreamless sleep.

VanSant wasted no time before placing his hand on her knee. He tilted his head back and soon joined her in slumber.

CHAPTER THREE

Mae reached her left hand up to the crook of her neck and wagged her head back and forth to relieve the stiffness from sitting in such an awkward position for hours. She straightened up, looked out the window, and saw the glow of morning brightening the sky outside. It took her a moment to realize Reginald's hand still rested on her leg. She lifted it gently and tucked it by his side. He made a soft sighing sound, but remained asleep. Surely it had been an unconscious move while he slept. Reginald would never be so bold. She looked at his handsome profile and smiled to herself. *I've only been out of the city a day and I already have a mature gentleman friend.* No sooner had she finished that thought when the train whistle blew and VanSant was jolted awake.

"We're pulling into the station, Mr. VanSant, I mean, Reginald. Good morning. Did you sleep well?"

"Very well. Thank you, Mae. And you?" He stretched both arms out to the side. His left arm brushed behind her head and extended past her arm. For a brief moment, Mae expected he might rest it on her shoulder. That thought sent chills down her spine and a flush up her neck to the top of her head. Instead, he returned both arms to his sides and shifted in the seat to get feeling back in his legs. "Well, I don't know about you, young lady, but I'm famished. A bit of breakfast sounds perfect. Won't you join me? I happen to know there is a small kitchen that serves wayfarers at this train station."

"That sounds lovely," Mae said. "But first ..." She didn't know how to say it without blushing.

VanSant immediately picked up on her discomfort and offered, "However, I must freshen up first. I will meet you inside shortly. How does that sound?"

"Wonderful."

Afterward, Mae, VanSant, and the rest of the passengers who could not afford the seventy-five cent meals served on the train returned to the car, discussing how many more hours it would be before they reached Chicago. VanSant informed them it would be another seventeen hours, with one more rest stop on the way.

He's so worldly. Mae felt privileged to be seen sitting with him. The other women in the immediate vicinity gave him quick, shy glances as the trip continued. Some of the men occupied their time playing cards and telling stories of previous trips they had made out West. Others smoked their cigars or pipes and napped periodically. Occasional snoring could be heard throughout the day. One little auburn-haired boy ran up and down the aisle making animal sounds—much to his mother's dismay. For some strange reason, Mae found his antics comforting. It reminded her of home. Of course, when she *was* home, this sort of behavior by her younger brothers would drive her to distraction. Here, on this train, however, it made her recognize people are the same everywhere, and that understanding calmed her growing fear of the unknown.

As the day wore on, VanSant became more and more familiar in the way he touched her arm, or hand, or her cheek, as he assured her that she would be the greatest performer to ever grace the stage at the Gem Theater. Mae began to recognize her own discomfort with his overt enthusiasm about her future. *After all, I'm only seventeen, just a girl. And he, well, he's a grown man. Why is he so interested in me, and not the others who look to be more his age?* She began to consider taking a seat elsewhere after the next rest stop. *You're being a silly little schoolgirl. What harm is there in having a well-traveled gentleman watching out for you? This is the adventure you wanted, remember?*

The unruly boy interrupted Mae's daydream by giving VanSant "the raspberries" and spraying spit into his face as he did. Her companion leapt to his feet, grabbed the young boy by the ear, and dragged him back to where his embarrassed mother sat, mortified by her son's behavior. All the while, VanSant cursed a blue streak of words Mae heard only once before in her life, after Mr. Goldstein's prize chicken was run over by Mr. Cohen's milk cart. To her mind, this episode did not appear to be nearly so serious!

Mae constricted her arms close to her sides upon his return. "Reginald, I don't like to see you so upset." Her throat tightened as she spoke and her voice cracked midsentence. In an attempt to disguise her own discomfort with his reaction, Mae lightly patted his arm. "Boys will be boys, you know."

VanSant's demeanor returned to calm and the redness left his face. "My apologies, Mae. I was raised by a very strict father who would never countenance such rude behavior. Like father, like son, I suppose." VanSant reached in his pocket for his pipe.

Mae stopped daydreaming about such things as diamond rings and strolling down the avenue on VanSant's arm. She became overtly interested in, and chatted about, the cloud formations, cornfields, turkey vultures circling, and anything else the train chugged past, to avoid more personal discussions with this stranger. After all, that's what he was, just a day ago. *I've got to remember what Papa told me—be careful of strangers. Don't tell them too much. Be polite, but keep to yourself as much as possible to stay safe. How could I have been so stupid?*

The rest of the trip to Chicago, Mae followed her father's advice. VanSant continued to try to draw her out, but she had learned her first lesson on being an adult out on her own, and did not respond in the childish way she had before. *Keep it polite, but reveal nothing personal to this man.*

She felt rather good about herself and relieved when the train's whistle blasted the air and the last hiss of steam wheezed from the engine. At last, the screeching of the wheels on the iron rails stopped at Wells Street Station, and the time came to bid her seatmate farewell. They exited the train, trailing behind their fellow passengers.

"Mae, allow me to carry your valise for you. I believe the connection to Whitewood, Dakota, leaves this evening at seven thirty, and if you like, we could share a meal before boarding." VanSant smiled as he took the bag from her.

"Thank you, but I think I can manage from here." Mae tried to wrest her suitcase back and added, "You're going to Whitewood too, Reginald?"

VanSant held firmly to the handle and jerked the bag away from her attempt to take it. Still smiling, he confirmed her fears. "Yes. Quite fortuitous, don't you agree?"

Mae had no idea what the word fortuitous meant, but managed a thin-lipped grin. "Yes. Quite."

Oh, Papa ... now what do I do? "Will you be staying in Whitewood, Reginald?" Mae said a silent prayer his answer would be yes. The aggressive way he controlled her suitcase made her feel more wary than his reaction to the little boy's antics.

"No. As a matter of fact, I'll be joining you on the stagecoach from there, all the way to Deadwood. So, you can rest assured, I will see you safely to your destination, Mae."

Her shoulders slumped, and she stopped walking. VanSant stopped a few steps ahead and turned back to see what she was doing. Mae made a halfhearted attempt at brushing the soot from the front of her long skirt to buy time to think. A solution presented itself.

"Supper sounds fine, Reginald. Thank you. But perhaps when we get back on the train, I should take a seat by another lady for the night. People are beginning to stare and God only knows what they must be thinking—a gentleman of your age, accompanying an obviously much younger girl, such as myself, when we are clearly not related. Don't you agree that arrangement would be best all around?" *Please God. Let him agree.*

"Not at all, Mae. Why, we can tell them I am your doting uncle. Surely they would not question our companionship after such an explanation." VanSant switched the suitcase to his left hand, clutched Mae's elbow with his right, and guided her into the station.

Mae's stomach churned through dinner as she made an attempt to be interested in VanSant's tales of the Wild West. He explained to anyone who would listen that he had agreed to accompany his niece at the behest of his sister. Reliving the touch of Reginald's hand on her knee the night before prevented her from paying much attention. The others at the long wooden table, who were on their first trip to the Hills country, continued questioning him about what they might expect. They were enthralled with his stories of the Indians and thieves they might encounter as they traveled by stagecoach to their final destinations. The men, in particular, wanted to hear if he'd ever been involved in a gun battle. The women stayed quiet, while giving each other frightened glances as they passed bowls of stew and plates of biscuits around the table.

VanSant and the other men drank whiskey and smoked their cigars and pipes while they waited for the engineer to announce "all aboard."

Mae tried to edge her way into a circle of women about to get on the train, but VanSant appeared out of nowhere, placed his hand on her shoulder, and said, "Come, my dear. It's time to board."

"Uh, yes, Uncle Reggie. Coming," was all Mae could manage. *I can do this. After all, I am an actress. I can pretend to be anyone I want.*

The train rumbled along through the pitch-black night, and again the monotonous side-to-side wobble of the car eventually rocked Mae into a fitful sleep next to her "uncle."

The next morning, filtered sunlight broke through the splotches of soot covering the window next to Mae, coaxing her awake, as the engine slowed on approach to the Union Depot in the Missouri Valley. She yawned dramatically, and wriggled more than necessary to purposely wake VanSant, who had interrupted her sleep repeatedly throughout the night with his gurgling drunken snore.

"Uncle! Uncle, we're here! Wake up!" Mae poked at his arm harder than necessary.

VanSant snorted, still half asleep, and shoved her hand away.

"Good morning!" Mae greeted him in her most dramatic, cheerful voice. She knew from experience with her real uncle that loud noises were most unwelcome when a man drank too much the night before. She smiled at her own cleverness.

CHAPTER FOUR

To everyone's great relief, the stagecoach encountered no outlaws or Indians as it wound its way through the jagged hills and began its descent into the valley of the frontier mining town of Deadwood, South Dakota. The smattering of people along their approach grew to be the pulsating heart of a swarm of humanity at the center of town. Horses, pack mules, rickety wagons, and rough-looking men with pickaxes slung over their shoulders crowded the dusty main road. Some of them cheered when they saw the coach arriving. To them it meant news from the outside world, and maybe some fresh female flesh.

Mae's heart was pounding with excitement as the driver pulled the reins back on the team of sure-footed horses that had brought her to her final destination. VanSant didn't bother to help her recover her suitcase from the pile of luggage the stagecoach driver tossed to the ground. But he wasted no time, after she retrieved it, in taking her arm and guiding her through the crowd to the entrance of a large two-story building across the street. Mae looked above the balcony, which spanned the entire front of the gray wooden structure, to the sign that read, "Gem Theater." *At last! Maybe now Uncle Reggie will let me be.*

VanSant ushered Mae through the swinging doors of the Gem saloon. "Al, this is Mae. Mae, meet Mr. Swearengen, the owner of this establishment."

"Well, well … what have we got here? Looks like you hit pay dirt in Philly, Reggie!" Al Swearengen slapped his back and added, "Well done! Grab yourself a drink." The proprietor turned to Mae and violated her without a touch—scanning every bit of her being with the blackest eyes Mae had ever seen. The heat rose from her breast, turning her freckled face the color of the satin dress worn by the painted lady at the bar. "Welcome to the Gem, little lady!" Swearengen tossed back the shot of whiskey he was gripping. "Alice, get your skinny ass over here and show our new girl to her quarters."

Mae scanned the dimly lit saloon. She had to suppress her gag reflex to the miasma of body odor, cigar smoke, stale beer, and cheap perfume. A flaking gilt-framed mirror provided a pockmarked reflective backdrop for the long mahogany bar. She turned around to locate the source of the out-of-tune tinkling of a piano and saw a disheveled blonde with ruby red lips and milky skin scurry off the lap of a scar-faced, bald man in the corner. The woman grabbed Mae's arm and shoved her toward the stairs to the right of the bar.

"I think there must be some mistake!" Mae tugged her arm from the blonde's grip. "I am Mae Steinberg—

Mae's Revenge

the actress," she added, with all the bravado she could muster. "I'm to be engaged at the Gem Theater, not a saloon." With both hands, she flipped her auburn curls to trail behind her shoulders. "Now, if you will direct me to the correct location, I will be much obliged."

The laughter that followed made Mae's heart stop. When she could breathe again, she looked to VanSant and asked, "What kind of a monster are you?" He responded with a nonchalant shrug. Tears began to dull her usually bright green eyes as the laughter grew louder.

"C'mon, girlie. We need to get you settled." The blonde took Mae's arm again, more gently this time, and led her up the stairs to a room at the end of the narrow hall. Mae squeezed past several scantily clad girls who appeared to be not much older than herself. *What are they all doing here? They can't all be actresses. And, why are they dressed like the jezebels Papa warned me to stay away from back in the city?*

The blonde swung open a door to reveal a bedroom with one small grimy window to the left, which peered out on the street in front of the Gem. Peeling, faded blue flowered wallpaper covered the room's bones. Centered on the far wall sat an iron spindle bed covered in a purple velvet spread that puddled onto the floor. There were two red satin pillows with gold fringe propped at the head of the bed. The only other furniture was a small walnut table crouching next to the bed and a tired vanity with a crescent-shaped bench tucked beneath.

"This is where you'll earn your keep," the blonde told her.

"My keep?"

"Well, you don't think you can live here for free, do ya? Say, kid, why did you think Reggie brought you here, anyway?"

"He didn't! *I* brought me here, after I saw the advertisement in the newspaper back home that said Mr. Swearengen was looking for actresses for his theater."

Alice shook her head and chuckled. "He's still using that old line? Sorry, kid. What'd you say your name is again?"

"Mae. Annie Mae Steinberg from Philadelphia. Nice to meet you, Alice." Mae offered her hand, but Alice did not oblige.

"Ya got any decent clothes in that bag of yours, Mae?"

"Certainly. I made quite a few skirts and shirtwaists at my family's shop. Papa is a tailor, and I've known how to sew from a very young age."

"Lemme see."

Mae opened the valise and began pulling gabardine skirts and polished cotton blouses from it. She spread them out on the bed and smoothed out the wrinkles for Alice to view.

"Oh fuck. You can't wear that stuff in front of Al! He'll throw you out on the street!"

Mae almost swallowed her tongue. She had never heard a lady use that disgusting word before. *Mama would faint if she knew her baby girl stood in the same room with someone who used that kind of language. It is kind of exciting, though, to think I appear grown up enough to hear words like that.*

"Then, what am I to do? These are the only clothes I have. Besides, I'll need decent attire to wear while I look for a position to earn the money I'll need to get back home. Clearly, I made a mistake coming here."

Alice picked up the blue shirtwaist Mae had worked so hard on, and attempted to rip off the ruffle-trimmed sleeves.

"What in the world are you doing? Do you know how long it took me to get those stiches just right?" Mae grabbed the blouse from her and clutched it to her chest.

Alice grabbed it back. "We're gonna make you fit in around here whether you like it or not. Al's not gonna let you go work for somebody else, and he runs things around here. I saw the way he looked at you. I've seen too many little girls tossed to the wolves in this rotten mining town. Besides, I think you've got potential. You'll be earning enough pretty soon to repay your family back East for what it cost them to send you. Isn't that what you want?"

"Of course. But what exactly will I be doing, Alice?"

"We're gonna make you so attractive to the Gem's clientele they'll be climbin' over each other to get to spend some time alone with you. Which is when you'll bring 'em up here."

"Up here? To my bedroom?" Her stomach climbed to her throat as she realized what Alice was telling her.

Mae's wide eyes betrayed her fear and Alice quickly changed the subject. "Now, help me get rid of these fuckin' sleeves!" She threw the plaid gingham shirtwaist at Mae's head, and then left the room.

Mae pulled the chamber pot from under the bed and gagged into it, but the effort proved useless. She managed to produce only a thin stream of bile, since she hadn't eaten all day.

Alice returned a few minutes later, armed with a large pair of shears. She removed the prim collar from the blue blouse, cut off seven of the top buttons, and tossed it to Mae. "Here, put this on for tonight. We'll take care of the rest of this tomorrow. Al won't expect you to work the room on your first night here, so get changed and come down to the kitchen for some supper."

Puddles of tears filled Mae's eyes.

Alice recognized the familiar anguish and put her arm around Mae's shoulder. "It's alright, kid. It's not so bad once you get used to it. And some of these bums aren't as rough as they look. Now, hurry up. Get changed." Alice left her alone.

Mae wiped her eyes and looked at herself in the small silvered mirror of the worn walnut vanity cowering in the corner of the room. *Papa would lock me in my room for the rest of my life if he could see me now. Hmm ... I wonder if I tucked these corners under here.* Mae created a wide V at the top of her blouse, exposing more of herself to the world than she ever had before. *Yes, that's better. Looks more like Alice and the other girls.*

Mae made her way through the crowd of men in the bar downstairs, including "Uncle Reginald," with only a few awkward moments when one or two reached out to pat her behind. VanSant's disgusting laughter followed her. Grateful to find the kitchen still offering supper to the workers not otherwise occupied for the evening, Mae offered a smile to the room. No one spoke. No one gave her the slightest glance. They concentrated on finishing their food so they would not miss out on a big score for the night. The girls knew how angry Al got

Mae's Revenge

when they didn't turn more than one trick each night, and it was getting late. Alice was not there.

"Hello. I'm Mae, from Philadelphia." The cook grunted and poured some milk into a tin cup. Mae took the plate of hash and cup of milk the cook offered her, then sat at the long trestle table in the middle of the shabby room. The other two girls got up, piled their dishes on the counter by the sink, and scurried back out to the bar without a word.

Mae shoveled a forkful of hash into her mouth and followed up with a swig of milk. *Didn't realize how hungry I was, and this isn't half-bad.* As she prepared to take another scoop, she heard a soft cough and turned to see a young man step out of the shadow of the far corner of the room.

"I hope I didn't frighten you," he said. "You're new here, aren't you?"

Mae dropped her fork onto her plate and put her hands in her lap. "Yes. I arrived this evening."

"I'm sorry. I should introduce myself. My name is Milmott—Gus Milmott. I work here. I do the books for Al."

"Do the books?"

"Yes, I'm an accountant. Mind if I sit down?" He took a seat across the table. "What's your name?"

"Mae. Actually, Annie Mae."

"And do you have a last name, Actually Annie Mae?" He smiled.

Mae felt the warmth of her blood as it flooded her cheeks, "Steinberg. My last name is Steinberg."

Her heart skipped a few beats. *Such a smile. I've never seen such a smile. And that dark wavy hair, and those broad shoulders. Mae, get a hold of yourself! You're being ridiculous. Think of "Uncle Reggie." This man might be another charlatan. Haven't you gotten yourself into enough trouble?*

"Well, Annie Mae Steinberg, it's very nice to meet you."

You've got to keep your wits about you. Yes, he's very handsome. But that's what you thought about Reginald. Don't be a silly schoolgirl.

"Annie Mae? Can you hear me?" Gus snapped his fingers.

"What? I'm sorry, were you saying something, dear? I—I mean, Gus. Were you saying something, Gus?" Mae wanted to slide under the table onto the floor.

Gus laughed. "I guess your mind went on a little trip. Mine does that sometimes too. Nothing to be embarrassed about. Now, tell me, how did you happen to end up at the Gem?"

"I'm not really sure. It certainly wasn't my intention. I came here to become an actress on the stage." *How stupid that sounds now.* "But, under the circumstances, I suppose it was a ridiculous dream."

"Doesn't sound ridiculous to me. Everyone should have dreams. And you've certainly got the looks for it ... I'm sorry ... I mean you're a very pretty, ahem, pleasant-looking young woman. Any theater would be glad to have you as their star." Gus smiled again.

"Is there a theater in Deadwood? Or was that just another lie that horrible Mr. VanSant let me believe?"

"Oh, VanSant brought you?"

"Well, not exactly. I saw an advertisement in the Philadelphia newspaper. Philadelphia, that's where I'm from. Anyway, it said Mr. Swearengen was looking for actresses for the stage at the Gem Theater. I've always wanted to be one, so I left my whole family and all my friends and got on the train heading west. I met Reginald, I mean Mr. VanSant, as soon as I boarded."

"That sounds about right." Gus shook his head. "Go on."

"Do you mind if I eat while I tell you? I'm awfully hungry!"

"Not at all. Please take your time. I've got all night."

Mae swallowed another forkful and gulped some milk before continuing. "It was all very exciting at first. He treated me with respect and sounded very worldly. All the passengers around us found him most entertaining." She produced an unexpected, loud belch. *Oh no! What must he think of me?* Mae covered her mouth with both hands. "Please excuse me. Must be because I haven't eaten anything today, until now. I'm so embarrassed!"

Gus reached across the table, took her wrist, and lowered her left hand from her face. "You never have to be embarrassed about anything in front of me. You do believe that, don't you, Mae?" He gave her one of his wide smiles.

She melted at his touch. Gazing into his warm hazel eyes, Mae's muscles relaxed for the first time in days. "If my brothers had done that at home, Mama would have given them a slap and told them to leave the table. Good thing she's not here." As soon as the words left her mouth, Mae's throat tightened. *Oh, Mama—you know I didn't mean that.*

"I can't imagine anyone slapping you for anything, Mae. Now, tell me about your family."

She brightened at his comment. "Well, I have two brothers, younger than me, David and Solomon. They're always getting into trouble, but I think Papa favors boys. I spent all my time helping Mama in the shop. My father's a tailor, you see."

"A tailor in the city. That sounds wonderful. I've lived on a farm way out in the country most of my life. Pretty dull. That's why I headed west a couple of years ago. To see the world and have some excitement in my life."

Alice appeared at the door and announced, "C'mon, kid. Tomorrow's gonna be a long day. Better get some shut-eye!"

"Oh. I didn't realize the time. Please excuse me, Gus. I *am* quite tired." Mae smiled at her new friend and added, "Good night." She glanced over her shoulder. "I'll be right there, Alice."

Gus stood as Mae cleared her place at the table. When she'd finished, he took her hand in his and said, "I'll see you tomorrow, Mae. Get a good night's sleep." Then, more confidentially, he added, "If you need me, don't hesitate to ask. I know my way around Deadwood and the Gem."

Mae's brow pinched. *Not again! I don't need another uncle.* She pulled her hand away. "I'm sure I'll be just fine. Thank you."

She hurried through the Gem's mostly abandoned bar area and trod upstairs to her room. Mae rubbed her temples as she looked into the small mirror over the vanity. *I look like I've aged ten years. Oh Papa. Your little girl made a very big mistake. I hope you never have to know.*

She fell asleep trying to block the moaning sounds echoing down the hall, imagining what it might be like to be married to an accountant. *Especially an accountant*

Mae's Revenge

with such an amazing smile and gentleness. I feel like I've known him for years. Maybe this trip was meant to be.

Exhausted from her travels and all the excitement of the evening before, Mae slept until well after sunup the next day. Defiantly dressed in an unaltered shirtwaist and modest skirt, she skipped downstairs to the kitchen, hoping Cook was still serving breakfast. She found Alice finishing up a plate of flapjacks and gristly bacon.

"Alice, have you seen Gus this morning?" Mae said, while cleaning a section of the long scarred table with the wet cloth the cook tossed to her. "I thought I'd invite him to join me for breakfast."

"He's gone," Alice said. She removed her hand from her right eye and took another sip of coffee.

"What do you mean, gone?" Mae looked up from cleaning the table and gasped. "Oh my God! What happened to you?"

"It's nothin' I can't handle." Alice straightened up. "Just some drunk asshole last night. Don't worry about me, kid—I can take it."

"You want a raw steak to put on it? Mama always used raw meat when the boys got their eyes blackened."

"Nah. It'll fade. And I can cover it with face powder until it does. Al doesn't like his girls to look damaged."

"He doesn't, does he?" Mae shivered at the mention of Al, and got herself a cup of coffee. "Anyway, do you know where Gus went?"

"Don't tell me you're sweet on him already? Forget it, Mae. Don't go getting involved with any of Al's men.

You gotta stay free and clear to keep the customers happy."

"Don't be silly. I'm not sweet on anybody. I just liked talking with him is all. Do you know where he is or don't you?"

"Keep your shirt on. Yeah, I know. He went back home to Ohio to see his poor mother. He got a telegram early this morning that his father was killed. Something about an accident on the family farm. Told Al he'd be back in a couple of weeks."

If he left so early, I wonder how Alice knows what he told Al? Unless ... oh my.

"How sad." Mae shook her head, and then finished her coffee. "Alice, how long till the other girls stop giving me the cold shoulder? When I got close to a few of them in the hall, they turned away and whispered. I don't understand. I haven't done anything to them. I haven't been here long enough to make enemies. Kitty, I think that's her name, you know the one with the red hair and the enormous bosoms, actually laughed right in my face when I came downstairs this morning!"

"Don't take it personally, kid. They don't want to get to know you until they're sure you're one of them. You'll see. After tonight, they'll warm up."

That night, the drunken miner gripped her arm and dragged her upstairs to her room.

Now alone with him, Mae whimpered, trying to free herself from his grip. "Please, mister ... I—I mean Charlie." *If I talk nice to him, maybe he'll treat me kindly.* Mae forced herself to look into his bloodshot eyes. "I've never done anything like this before."

Mae's Revenge

Without acknowledging her pleas, the scruffy, toothless man with the sandpaper beard, in a scraping rasp of a voice, ordered her to shut up, shoved her backward onto the bed, and fell on top of her.

Mae turned her head away from his sweaty face and whiskey breath, and began to cry as he tore at her blouse, hiked up her skirt, and ripped away her bloomers. Charlie used his own legs as pliers to spread hers. He cursed to himself as he fumbled with the buttons on his fly and then with one brutal thrust he was inside her.

She bit her lip to prevent the scream of pain from escaping and covered her eyes with both hands. Her brain pounded inside her skull while their bodies bounced up and down on the screeching old iron bed frame. As Charlie's moaning crescendoed, the room swirled behind her clenched eyelids and then all went black.

As suddenly as it began, it ended. Mae was coaxed back to consciousness by the cool wet spot on the bedsheet beneath her. She slowly opened her eyes to discover her abuser had left her all alone to face her shame. Her first experience was over. *I must have passed out. Oh God, I hurt!* She reached down between her thighs, squinted to look at her hand in the dull gaslight, and saw blood on her fingers. Tears formed salty rivers down her cheeks to her quivering chin. She rolled onto her side, wrapped her belly with her arms, drew her legs up to her chest, and rocked back and forth. A pile of crumpled bills on the nightstand were not enough to console her. *Mama. Papa. How can I ever face you again?* She descended into a fitful slumber, sure she never would.

CHAPTER FIVE

Over the next several weeks, without any word from or about him, thoughts of Gus began to fade. Mae gave up on any hope of returning home. She got used to sitting on strangers' laps, dancing with them, drinking with them, cursing with them, and in general adopting the mantle of being one of Al's girls. She'd been in the middle of, or witnessed, at least three bloody barroom brawls. One brutal fight spilled out onto Main Street, where the losing combatant ended up with a bullet in his head. It was the first time Mae saw the violent death of a human being up close. She replayed the episode over and over in her mind, as if it happened yesterday:

"Get your ass upstairs, Philly!" Al called her that whenever she made him angry. "But clean up that vomit before you go. It's not good for business for the gents to see you in such a state!"

Never saw so much blood pour out of a person! Mae continued to wretch as she sopped the spit up with the bar rag.

Mae's Revenge

"What the hell's the matter with you, girl? Never seen a dead man before?" Al smacked her face. "Snap out of it!" He told her to take the rest of the night off. Not out of kindness, but because she kept gagging and spewing, and that was bad for business.

Despite her weak stomach, Mae became a popular pick with the locals. Most of them didn't want her face damaged, and on more than one occasion, a man would step in on her behalf if someone threatening from the outside showed up and started giving her a hard time. The other girls had accepted her as one of them. Life was as good as it was going to get in Deadwood.

Two months passed and summer arrived with a furnace blast, baking the earth and people alike. Gus wiped the dripping sweat from his forehead and glared at her thin, pale face. "Mae? What the hell happened to you?" He almost didn't recognize his young friend when he saw her for the first time since his return from Ohio.

The underside of Mae's long tresses stuck to the sides of her face and neck from perspiration and she tried to conceal her split mouth with lip rouge. Unfortunately, last night no one had stepped up to defend her. She held her hand over the swollen corner of her mouth, and despite the pain, tried to greet him with a welcoming smile. "I'm so glad you're back, Gus. How is your mother? I was sorry to hear about your father. How are you?" She hung her head and weakly spoke to the floorboards. "You've been gone so long."

Gus grabbed her by the shoulders, and then lifted

her chin to the flickering gaslight of the wall sconce. "Who did this to you? Was it VanSant? Tell me, Mae!"

"No. It wasn't him. He headed back East right after you left. It doesn't matter. Please, Gus. Let it go." Mae tucked her chin from his hand and looked away from the light. "You must tell me all about your family and your travels. I've been conjuring you in all kinds of adventurous situations. Let's go to the clearing behind the stables. We can pack a picnic lunch and you can tell me all about it. I don't have to work until after four o'clock."

"Work? Is that what you call it now? My God, Mae—what happened to you while I've been gone? I thought you'd get a position with *The Daily Pioneer* or working for Farnum at the Grand Central."

"Al wouldn't let me because—" Mae started to explain when they were suddenly interrupted.

"Hey, Annie Mae, is this the guy you've been cryin' over?" Mildred, one of the new girls, asked as she pushed between them in the upstairs hall. She made sure to rub her chest against his as she squeezed past. Over her shoulder, she added, "Don't blame ya, kid—he's a looker!"

Despite the way she had been spending her nights while Gus was away, Mae reverted to her innocent blush. Something about him made her feel pure again. *How is that possible? He makes me feel clean in spite of all the shameful things I've done.* Mae immediately changed the subject back to him to get past the embarrassment, as she headed downstairs. "C'mon, Gus let's get some sandwiches from Cook and have that picnic. I'm sure you have lots of stories to tell!"

Mae's Revenge

Gus took Mae's hand as they stepped through the saloon's swinging doors onto the thoroughfare in front of the Gem. After the last rainstorm slathered the street in mud, the scorching sun had created cement-like ruts in the roadway from wagon wheels and horse traffic. Mae clung to his arm as they navigated the bumpy road to the other side. The pair went behind the livery stable, where they spread their picnic lunch on a grassy patch under the canopy of an enormous oak.

Gus sat cross-legged on the grass next to her. "Here, take a swig of this. It'll numb the pain in that lip of yours." He twisted the cork out of a bottle of whiskey he had pulled from his jacket pocket and handed it to her.

Mae took a swallow and scrunched up her face as if she had bitten into a lemon. "I don't think I'll ever get used to that stuff." She wiped her mouth gingerly and handed the bottle back to him. "Now, tell me what happened at home."

Gus took a deep gulp of the whiskey before beginning. "Well, you know my father died, right?"

"Yes, Alice told me."

"Anyway, I stuck around long enough to bring in a couple of hired hands to help Ma with the farm. I couldn't believe how many men I had to turn away because I knew they were up to no good and woulda taken advantage of her."

"I'm sure she was happy to have you home, Gus. But I have to admit I'm glad to have you back in Deadwood. The other men around here only want to strike it rich, get drunk, and fuck." As soon as the word passed her lips, she blushed. "Sorry ... when in Rome, as they say."

Gus chuckled and gulped another shot of whiskey. "Want some more? It'll help you relax, and then you can tell me what else has been going on around here while I've been gone." He uncrossed his legs and leaned back on his right elbow, scooted his body closer to hers, and flashed one of his mesmerizing smiles.

Mae rejected the whiskey in favor of the sarsaparilla Cook had put in a jug for them. Doc had urged the girls to drink that particular beverage often, to help protect them from diseases peculiar to their line of work. Most of the other girls paid him no mind, but Mae was determined to remain as healthy as possible for the "someday" when she would escape this dreary existence.

"What did your Ma and Pa say when they found out you're not an actress?" Gus asked.

"I haven't told them." Mae shifted away from him, and looked up at the umbrella ribs of drooping oak leaves as she continued. "When I write, I tell them the basics. I'm eating well. I've made a lot of friends. The scenery is amazing. I have enough work to support myself. And I fib about the performances I've done. They need never know the truth." She dropped her gaze, picked at her fingers, and added, "It would break their hearts."

Gus took her hand and squeezed it. "I'll never tell," he said, and grinned up at her.

Mae pulled her hand away and smacked his arm. "Thanks a lot!"

They spent the remainder of their time together eating, drinking, laughing, and flirting. Then came the awkward time when they knew they had to return to the Gem. Four o'clock in the afternoon had arrived,

Mae's Revenge

so Gus reluctantly kissed her cheek before Mae went to her room to apply some fresh lip rouge and pin her ginger-colored hair up into a pile of seductive curls.

CHAPTER SIX

Mae and Gus continued their platonic relationship for the next several months. Without discussing it, it appeared they both wanted their friendship to stay separate and apart from the depravity going on around them. Gus reluctantly concentrated on making sense of Al's questionable financial records, while Mae tolerated the ugliness of the Gem's patrons. Gus knew, deep in his gut, he would not be able to look the other way forever when it came to Mae's "work" because he was falling in love with her. He didn't dare express his feelings to her until he'd accumulated enough money to be able to marry and move away from Deadwood.

Most nights he would nurse his whiskey, stare into the mirror behind the bar, clench and unclench his fists, and watch her being fondled by some drunk miner until, as it always happened, they would disappear up the staircase. On more than one occasion, he considered picking one of the other girls for his own pleasure, in order to give Mae a taste of his pain. He didn't follow through, though, after reminding himself she had no choice. Gus witnessed firsthand a few of the beatings Al dished out to girls who refused the work. He had also heard the sordid stories of more than one suicide. He would never wish that on Mae.

"What are you talking about, Gus? Of course I don't enjoy it!" Mae stopped walking and turned her back on him. "I can't believe you would say such a thing. Don't tell me you're jealous!"

Gus moved around her and cupped her chin with his hand, to talk face to face. "I don't get it. Why can't you say 'no' once in a while? Tell 'em you're sick or something."

Mae pushed his hand away. "You know Al wouldn't give a shit if I *were* sick. He'd still take his cut, from my savings, and then I'd never get away from this hellhole." She turned and resumed walking in the direction they were originally going.

It took Gus a minute to catch up to her brisk pace. He knew he crossed some invisible line and tried to work out how to make things between them better again.

"You know, Mae, I've got some savings too. And I was thinking ... maybe if we put our savings together ... we could both get out of here. What do you think about that?"

Mae's heart skipped a beat. *If you only knew. Dreaming about escaping this filthy snake pit is the only thing that keeps me sane.* "How much have you saved? I've got thirteen dollars and fifty-seven cents."

"Wow. That much? That's a lot for a prosti … I mean someone in your line of work."

"Yes. Well, I don't tell Al about *every* penny I earn." Mae held her head a bit higher as they continued down the street, proud of her own cleverness.

"Annie Mae, if Al ever finds out you're stiffing him, I don't like to think about what he might do to you!"

"Don't be a pinhead, Gus. He'll never know, unless *you* tell him." Mae took his arm, looked up at his concerned expression, batted her lashes, and pursed her lips into a pout. "You wouldn't, would you?"

"Of course not! You must know I never would."

"So, you didn't answer me. How much do you have stashed away?"

Gus hesitated. "Let's just say, not enough. Not yet, anyway. C'mon, let's stop talking about saving money. I thought we were supposed to be enjoying a few hours off." Gus took Mae's hand and guided her into the dry goods store to see what new items the stage had delivered the day before. "Go ahead. Pick something. After all, it *is* your birthday. Eighteen is a very special age."

"I'm surprised you can remember that far back!" Mae laughed at her own joke.

"Very funny. I remember it like it was yesterday. I'm only twenty-three, ya know!"

Each night that passed made Gus more desperate, until early one morning he decided he couldn't take it anymore. Once he knew her latest visitor had staggered out of the saloon, he stuffed the last two embezzled twenties into his boot and headed upstairs to rescue Mae.

Mae was already half asleep as she ushered him into her room, where Gus's proposal completely eluded her comprehension.

"What the hell are you talking about, Gus? I can't just pack up and leave that fast! Al would kill me if I took off without letting him know ... wait a minute ... did you say, marry?"

Gus bobbed his head.

Wide awake now, Mae threw herself at him, wrapped her arms around his neck, and began kissing his whole face.

"Does this mean yes?"

"Yes! Yes! Yes! Of course, I'll marry you! Give me ten minutes to pack my bag!"

"Okay ... but be quiet about it. I don't want anyone tipping Al off before we get away from here. The stage leaves soon, and I want us to be on it."

"Where are we going, Gus? Why can't we get married right here?" *Mae paused and envisioned herself surrounded by the other girls all jealously whispering while she, with a garland of flowers crowning her head, said "I do" in response to the preacher. Gus, of course, would gaze down at her with loving adoration as he placed the shiny gold band on her finger. The magical kiss that followed would draw gasps from those in attendance. Surely, there would never be a more romantic wedding!*

"Mae! Annie Mae! Stop daydreaming, please. We don't have much time. We've got to get out of here fast!"

Mae's mind returned to the present and she sprang into action, pulling her valise from under her bed. She haphazardly shoved all of her meager belongings into it. "But, Gus, why do we have to leave in such a hurry?"

"I'll tell you on the way. Right now, we don't have time to chew the rag … please, Mae, get a wiggle on!" Gus helped Mae secure the straps on her bag while pushing down hard on its bulging sides.

"There, that's it," Mae said. "I'm ready, Gus. Can I go say good-bye to Alice?"

"No, no one, Mae. We've got to get outta here, c'mon."

The couple descended the stairs as quiet as possible, while the rest of the Gem staff and clientele slept. Chilling darkness greeted them as they made their way out into the cold winter wind.

PART TWO

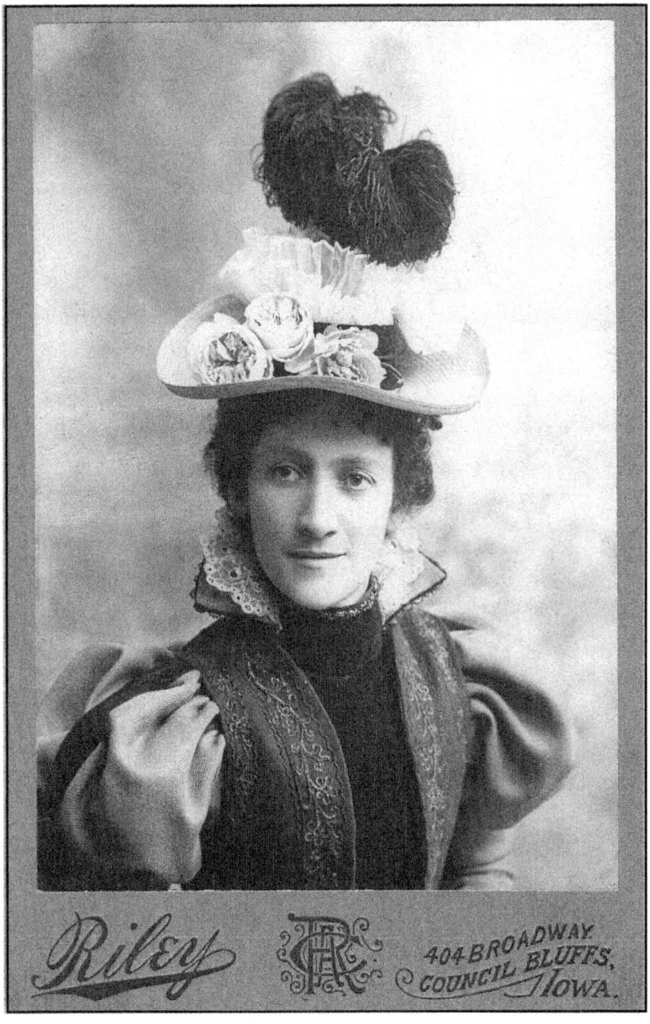
Riley
404 BROADWAY
COUNCIL BLUFFS,
IOWA.

CHAPTER SEVEN

Annie Mae Steinberg became Mrs. Gus Milmott as soon as they arrived in Council Bluffs, Iowa. No garland of flowers crowned her head, and Mae suspected the band Gus placed on her finger contained more tin than silver, but she didn't mind. She waited until they were settled to ask about the stolen money. Gus explained he had taken only enough for the two of them to start life some place far enough away from the Gem that Al wouldn't catch up with them. She didn't press any further. Mae was grateful to have a fresh start.

It didn't take long for her new husband to find work as a bookkeeper at the dry goods store, and the Revere House, the boardinghouse where they found shelter on Broadway, certainly proved to be more pleasant than living under Al's thumb at the Gem. Mae and Gus shared the sixteen-room house with fifteen other boarders, and they were happy to afford the sixteen dollars a month.

Mae's Revenge

Mae made it a point to become acquainted with some proper ladies in town, and joined the local theater company, working as a seamstress. It was on one of her walks to the theater that she spied her. At first she wasn't sure, but when the woman came closer, Mae recognized the red hair and large bosoms. *It can't be ... not here! Kitty Reynolds from the Gem?*

"Mae? Is that you? I don't believe it!" Kitty bellowed from ten feet away.

"Kitty? What in the world are you doing in Iowa?" Mae said. She looked around to see if anyone she knew was nearby. *No one ... thank God.*

"Found me a fella and hightailed it outta Deadwood as soon as he got out of the hoosegow! Guess we both had the same idea, huh, Mae?"

"Gee whiz! What was he in jail for, Kitty? Not murder, I hope!"

"'Course not. Chiseled some big mouth outta his money during a friendly little poker game. Turned out the fella was a gol-dang US marshal. Accused my man of cheating and had him locked up for a few nights. When he got out, we skedaddled when Al wasn't around."

"Well, I'm glad you got away safely. But I must be going. Have to get to work." Mae touched Kitty's arm and added, "You take care now," before resuming her walk to the theater.

"Yeah. Swell seeing you, Mae. Maybe we can get together some time." When Mae didn't respond, Kitty knew that would never happen. She continued down the avenue in the opposite direction, looking down at her feet, not knowing or caring where she would end up. Her "fella" had stormed out on her last night and made off with what little savings she had.

L.C. Bennett Stern

Two weeks later, Mae read in *The Daily Nonpareil*:

Kitty Reynolds, from Deadwood, South Dakota, aged thirty, most recently staying at 141 East Pierce Street, committed suicide by morphine overdose. Body found by Patrolman Wolff and taken to Lunkley's Undertaking Rooms. Some of those who shared her life of shame on the "Row" collected enough for a burial at Fairview Cemetery. No known relatives.

Mae looked up from the newspaper. Her face was paper white. "Gus, do you remember Kitty from the Gem?"

"Yeah. Wasn't she the redheaded one? With the big—"

"Yes. I can't believe it—I just saw her on the street a couple of weeks ago. She's dead! It says here she killed herself with morphine. I feel terrible."

"Why do you feel terrible? You didn't kill her. That sort of thing happens all the time to her type."

"Her type?" The color returned to Mae's face.

"Now, wait a minute. I wasn't talking about you. You're different. Some of those girls ... that's all they ever knew how to do." Gus walked over to Mae and kissed her cheek. You're an accomplished woman. You sew. You paint ..."

"All right. All right. You talked your way out of it this time." Mae arched one eyebrow and smiled.

The letters Mae sent home to Philadelphia were full of what she believed to be truth—at last.

Mae's Revenge

Dear Papa,

Tell Mama that Gus says he might bring me home for a time, next spring. I would love to see all of you ...

Dear Papa,

Tell Mama that Gus says we will be raising our children in a proper house. He hopes we will have a gaggle of kids ...

"So, what did the doctor say?" Gus greeted Mae at the door.

"He said I'm perfectly healthy and there's no reason we can't have a houseful of children—but these things take time and we have to be patient." Mae looked away from the obvious disappointment shadowing his face.

"Patient? My Ma had three kids by the time she reached your age. I don't understand."

"I'm not an old woman, you know. I still have plenty of time." Mae became annoyed. She took off her coat and hat and dished out the stew she brought up to their room for supper. "I told the landlady I wasn't feeling well, so she said we could eat up here. Go wash your hands. I bought your favorite peanut butter cookies from Mrs. Lucasi on my way home." She wanted to change the subject and hoped the bribe would work. It did.

"Thanks, Annie Mae." Gus looked into his empty bowl. "I can't believe I ate so much." He leaned back and patted his stomach. "But it's been a long day, and I need to get some sleep." He winked at Mae.

"Some sleep, huh?"

Gus grabbed one more cookie and held it between his teeth as he untied his shoes, kicked them off, unbuttoned his trousers, and tossed them into the corner by the bed. He finished eating the cookie before removing his shirt, and it joined his pants in a pile on the floor.

Mae dutifully gathered his clothes and hung them on the hook by the two-tiered washstand.

By now, Gus was settled into bed anxiously waiting for her to undress. He patted the spot next him. "C'mon, Mae. Let's make some babies."

CHAPTER EIGHT

As time went by, winter in Iowa once again turned brutal, and Mae's letters home dwindled to a trickle. There were no trips back East, and the gaggle of children—a fading dream.

"**Amanda, would** it be okay if I took the leftover canvas from the prop cupboard? And I saw some brushes and half-used paints in there too. May I have them?" Mae and the theater manager where she worked were good friends by now, which meant Mae knew the answer before Amanda spoke.

A short, plump woman with apple cheeks, the manager had a head of frizzled silver hair she let flow loosely down her back. Mae admired Amanda's artistic abandon when it came to fashion, with her flowing colorful scarves and large sparkling rings adorning all but her chubby thumbs. She also enjoyed hearing her full-throated laughter at the latest bawdy joke.

"Certainly, my dear." Amanda looked up from the ticket stubs she was sorting at her desk. "What do you have in mind?"

"My evenings are much too quiet, and I've been thinking a hobby might fill the time." A bit self-conscious, Mae decided she owed her friend an explanation. "I used to draw a lot when I was a girl, but I never tried oils until I started helping with the stage backdrops here. I want to try my hand at still lifes. What do you think?"

"I say that's an absolutely marvelous idea, and take anything from the cupboard you might need. If you decide to do living things instead of dead fruit, I'll be happy to pose for you! I do still have some life in this old girl's figure, you know!" Amanda threw her head back and let loose one of her signature laughs.

These days, Gus arrived home late more often than not. Mae came to expect the smell of whiskey on his breath, but was more alarmed at how rough their waning sex life became. His moods were unpredictable and frightening. Mae dreaded sundown. After their evening meal, she would concentrate on her paintings while he drank, and then she'd tiptoe around after he fell asleep. He only hit her hard that one time, but she told herself it was the drink—not really him. Until it happened again last week.

Mae's Revenge

March 26, 1900

Dear Papa,

It is snowing here again and I cannot bear much more of this wind. How is your weather in Philadelphia? I have some good news. Tell Mama that Gus says he will be getting a raise soon, and I have started putting some money aside again for a trip East ...

The door crashed shut as Gus swooped into the room. Mae's spine shot ramrod straight at the sound. She swung around from the rickety writing table so fast she knocked the bottle of ink over, splashing the blue liquid onto her lap and the floor. Still clutching her fountain pen, she cowered at the blistering rage on her husband's face. Her hand automatically cradled her still tender, bruised left cheek.

"That bastard fired me!" Gus shouted. "Accused me of stealing from him!" He grabbed the bottle of whiskey from the cupboard hanging over the tired washstand in the corner and took a long swallow right from the bottle before continuing his rant. "Son-of-a-bitch didn't even give me a chance to explain what happened to the missing money. Told me to clear out, right then and there!" He took another swallow.

"What do you mean? Stealing? Oh Gus, not again!" Mae's stomach cramped and her head began to pound.

Gus flopped into the one upholstered seat they had and gulped the whiskey again before wiping his mouth on his coat sleeve.

Mae remained riveted to her chair, staring at her husband. *God forgive me ... I've married a thief! The sheriff is probably on his way. Where will we go this time? I'd better start packing ...*

Her imaginings were interrupted when Gus jumped to his feet and stomped across the room. He snatched up the bonnet she recently bought to have her photograph taken in, to send to her parents. "Why the hell do you always spend my pay on such ridiculous shit?" He shook the bonnet at her. "Do ya think you're some kind of a lady? Well, you're not! You'll never be anything but the whore I married!" With that, he threw it at her head, but missed as he swigged more whiskey from the bottle gripped in his left hand. The fancy straw, flowered, and feathered hat landed in the spilled ink at her feet.

Mae sobbed and cursed him under her breath while trying to save the bonnet from the puddle of blue, but it was no use. "It's ruined!" she blubbered.

Gus dismissed her with a wave of his arm, turned, and put his foot through her most recent painting, which she had propped against the coal scuttle to dry. He grumbled something Mae couldn't make out and collapsed into the chair to finish off the whiskey.

Mae refrained from reacting to the damaged canvas and turned her back on him, so he couldn't see her tears of outrage. *Why don't you just leave? I'd be happier on my own. Maybe you'll die in your sleep. I could take the money you stole and go home to my family—to the people who truly love me.*

You would need an ax to cut through the silence that suffocated the room.

Later, when Gus's drunken snoring became constant, Mae crumpled the letter she had been writing, threw it into the trash bucket, and began gathering her few belongings. She piled them into the valise she had

Mae's Revenge

stored under the sagging yellow pine bed pressed against the far wall. After drying her bonnet the best she could, she placed it into her hatbox and quietly put both bags by the door. She knew when Gus awoke, they would have to move quickly. *Maybe we can go someplace warm. I saw pictures of California in the Ladies Home Journal at the theater. If I'm nice to him when he wakes up, maybe he'll take me there. I wonder if he stole enough money to travel that far?*

Mae lay on her side diagonally across the bed and pulled half of the frayed multicolored Log Cabin quilt over her hip and legs. With the deflated feather pillow tucked under her head, she dozed off into a restless sleep.

"Mae ... Mae. Wake up." Gus gently shook her shoulder to prod her awake. "I'm sorry. You know I didn't mean to ruin your silly hat. You know that, don't you? I was just mad at that stupid bastard ... not you ... never you. C'mon, Mae, wake up. We gotta get a move on."

Mae withdrew deeper into the pillow to escape his stale whiskey breath on her neck. "I know. I know. Give me a minute and I'll make some coffee." As he backed away, she stretched her arms over her head and yawned long and low. *California. He's got to take me to California. I need to see the sun and be warm. He'll be different out there. We'll be happy again.*

"C'mon, lazy bones. I put some more coal in the potbelly so it's ready for ya. How about that coffee? We've gotta skedaddle." Gus lightly smacked her ass and chuckled.

PART THREE

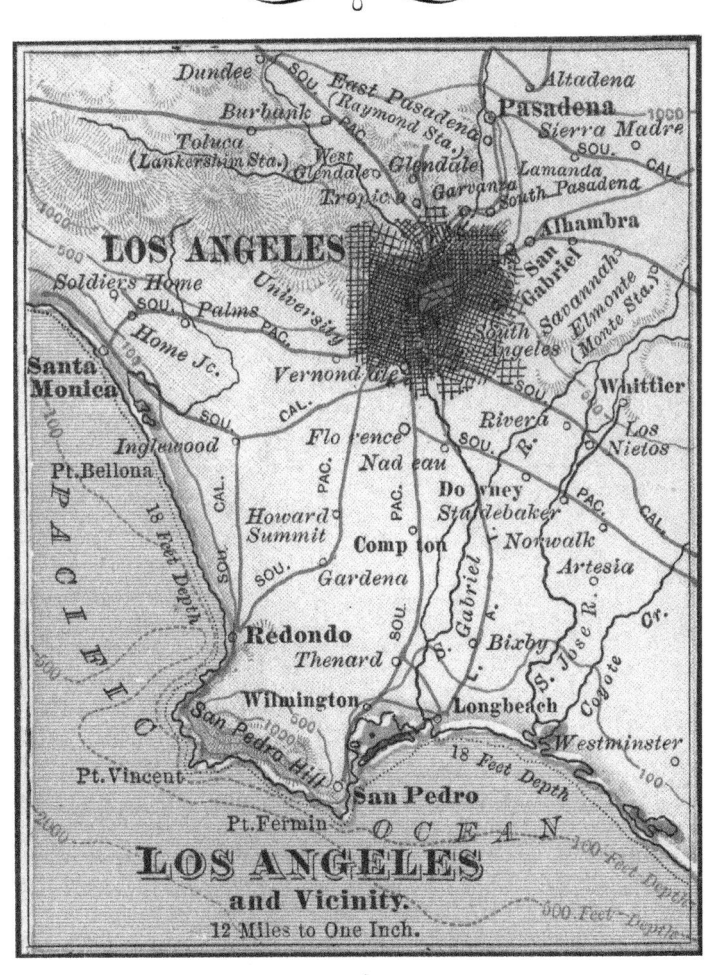

Los Angeles, 1900

CHAPTER NINE

The trip west on the Union Pacific and Central Pacific rails treated Mae and Gus to some of the most spectacular natural scenery either of them had ever seen. Rumbling through desolate plains in Nebraska, majestic mountains of Colorado, Utah's rugged terrain, and then Nevada's deserts and mountain peaks to the West Coast, had Mae feeling exhausted and happy. She smiled as they reached their last stop of the week. *Oh my! Los Angeles. I can feel the warmth already. I wonder how far away the Pacific Ocean is ... hope we get to see it today. Hello, California! Nice to meet you at last!*

They followed the other passengers through the crowds at the depot, pushing and shoving, until they got outside. Gus tossed their bags in the dirt in front of the station's wooden walkway. "Wait here. I'll be back in a couple of minutes," he told her, and headed to the Union Bar and Cafe across the road. He had spotted the sign when the train pulled in.

Mae's Revenge

"But shouldn't we find a room first?" Mae called after him.

"Just wait there."

"But, Gus, we just got here …" Mae's voice trailed off in defeat. She began to organize their belongings.

"I won't be long," Gus called over his shoulder and gave her a quick smile.

Mae shook her head and plopped down on the edge of the walkway in front of the station. With her elbows resting on her knees and her head cradled by her palms, she settled in to wait. And wait. *Not gonna see the ocean today, that's for sure. But look at that lady's bonnet. I never saw one with that many ostrich feathers before. Wonder if it came from a local shop? Probably out of a catalog from back East. New York designs all the best fashions. Wonder if she'd let me paint her in her fancy hat sometime?* She daydreamed about the still lifes she painted during their time in Iowa. The ones Gus wouldn't let her bring along. *It was okay for him to send the one with the pink roses to his mother, though!* Painting, she discovered, calmed her nerves after his drunken outbursts. Mae looked across the avenue and sighed. *Looks like I'm gonna need more canvas and brushes.* She frowned, straining to see if there were any rooming houses nearby. The fading light made that impossible. Mae leaned against one of the depot's upright supports as the evening wore on.

"Are you okay, ma'am? Are you sick? Do you want me to fetch the doc?" A boy, who looked to be about ten years old, stood directly in front of her in the road, with a scruffy brown three-legged dog at his side.

Startled, Mae said, "Oh, no thank you, young man. Just waiting for my husband. I'm sure he'll be along soon."

"Well, if ya need anything, I can fetch my Ma."

"No, no, I'm fine, but thank you." Mae smiled, then reached out and scratched behind the dog's ear. "You two better run along. It's getting late and your Ma will be worried. I'm fine, really." They took off into the twilight, the scruffy dog hobbling along behind his master, and for the first time in a long while, Mae wondered how her brothers were doing back home.

At last, her eyelids fluttered shut, and her head began to bob onto her chest as she gave in to weariness and napped.

"What the hell are you doing? Do you want to get robbed?" Gus yanked her by the arm to pull her up.

"No! Of course not," Mae mumbled, prying away from his grasp and the stench of his breath. She shivered in the night air and rubbed her eyes into focus. "What time is it?"

"About ten. C'mon, I got us a room." Gus picked up two of their bags, throwing one over his shoulder. "Grab that thing." He pointed at her hatbox.

Mae trudged behind as he staggered for what seemed like hours until, at last, they reached their destination—a ramshackle rooming house at the edge of the business district.

"Barkeep told me about this place. Said it's cheap enough for us."

Mae followed him into a dark, musty foyer. She glanced at the filthy splintered floorboards and the cobwebs draping the corners of the ceiling. *Oh, I'll bet this costs a pretty penny.*

Mae's Revenge

An ancient, humped-back woman with the longest white hair Mae had ever seen limped to the counter when Gus smacked the bell. "Keep your shirt on! How many nights?" she barked.

"How much?"

"Eight a month. Cheap at half the price!"

"How much for a week?" he slurred.

"Two-fifty."

"Make it a week for two dollars and we'll take it."

"You're a real corker, ain't ya? But what the hell, it's late. Cough it up."

"Here ya go," Gus said. He pulled cash from his jacket pocket and counted out two one-dollar bills.

In the dim glow from the single electric bulb dangling overhead, Mae saw he had a wad of bills, which he quickly shoved back into his jacket. *With all that money, why do we have to stay in this awful place? We passed a wonderful hotel right down the street from the station. I bet they had maid service and running hot water too.* The old woman interrupted her musings.

"Through that door, up the stairs, third room on the left." The rooming house matron pointed and then disappeared behind the moth-eaten, pale jade curtain serving as the doorway to her private quarters.

Mae wanted to cry, but was too played out to produce tears. Her dreams of starting fresh in this land of sunshine drained away more and more with each creaking step, as she followed Gus up the narrow staircase and down the stinking hallway to their room.

CHAPTER TEN

Gus used his charm to convince the old battle-ax who ran the rooming house to agree to a weekly rent of two dollars by telling her they would be moving on soon. Soon could not come soon enough, as far as Mae was concerned. The smell of stale urine seeped beneath their door from the hallway, and she recognized the sound of rats scrambling down the stairs on more than one occasion. On the positive side, by the end of their first week in Los Angeles Mae had found work at a tailoring shop in the center of town. There, she was immediately befriended by a coworker named Claire, who was barely a year her senior, at the age of thirty-one.

"Gus, we've got to get out of here. I can't take it much longer." Mae slammed the door, removed her shawl, and hung it over the bed's footboard.

"Wha—what?" He slumped forward in the chair where he had passed out the night before. He tried to make sense of the time on his pocket watch, but his bloodshot eyes would not focus. "What're ya doin' home so early?"

"Don't tell me you slept the whole day away! You promised you were going to look for work. It's after six." She slammed a pot onto the wood-burning stove, grabbing her apron from a nail in the wall. Her anger pounded in her chest as she pried open a can of pork and beans for their supper.

"Honest, Mae, I was going to look for work, but I don't feel so good." Gus rubbed his belly and belched loud and long. "See?" As he moved, he accidentally kicked over the empty whiskey bottle at his feet.

"Pick that up and throw it out this minute!" She was exhausted and depressed. "I don't understand. I thought when we moved out here we would make a fresh start, but things have just gotten worse." Mae shook her head as she stirred the pot. "Have I done something to make you angry with me?"

"No, Mae. It's not you. It's me. I always set my sights too high, I guess." He scratched his crotch. "By now I expected we'd be settled in some nice little house with a bunch of kids running around. But, well …"

"Well what? Are you blaming *me* for us not having any children? I told you the doctor said I'm perfectly healthy—there's no reason I can't have them! Oh my God. Is that why you hate me?" Her eyes blurred with tears and she dropped the spoon into the pot. "Ouch! Shit!" Mae cursed as she retrieved it and wiped the handle off on her apron.

"I don't hate you, Mae. You know I could never hate you." Gus rolled his head from shoulder to shoulder to ease the stiffness and scuffed over to her at the stove.

He put his arms around her waist from behind and kissed her ear.

Mae pulled away from his hot, putrid breath, and continued to stir the beans.

"C'mon, Annie Mae, don't be like that. I'm sorry. Truly I am. I promise—tomorrow I'll go find some kind of work." He rubbed the back of his neck. "There must be something for a man of my talents at that insurance office over by the train station. I'll go there first thing in the morning. And when I get my first pay, I'll take you out for a proper meal." He turned her around, lifted her chin, and gave her that smile that still melted her heart.

Brightening, Mae offered, "Or maybe Farmers and Merchants Bank on Main Street. Perhaps you might try both tomorrow. Will you, Gus? Please?" She ladled some beans into a bowl, handed him a spoon, and said, "Here, you need to eat something." She pulled off the end from the loaf of bread she bought on her way home from work and handed him that, too. "And promise me we'll get out of this rat-trap as soon as you have a job." Mae sat with her bowl of beans in her lap. "I want to move closer to the center of town, so I don't have to walk so far to work. A place with some proper furniture so we can eat at a table like human beings! My friend, Claire, at work, told me there are lots of rooms to let in those big old houses downtown. I know you have the money. I saw that roll of bills you shoved into your pocket the night we came to this horror. You couldn't possibly have drunk it *all* away."

Gus started to protest between mouthfuls, but Mae had heard it all before. *And I still haven't seen the ocean. It can't be that far. Maybe I'll go by myself, if Mr. Shoemacher ever gives me a day off.* Mae stopped her daydreaming

Mae's Revenge

and got up to open the window more. The whole room reeked of whiskey, and it was ruining her appetite. She glanced at Gus before continuing to eat. *Look at him. He used to be so handsome. Before the alcohol got such a hold on him. It's getting so I can't remember why I ever married him. Stop it, Mae. Don't be a lunkhead. He's your husband and you know you still love him.*

That night, for the first time since they arrived in California, Mae and Gus genuinely made love. As he held her afterward, Mae snuggled into his chest and smiled dreamily until her tired limbs relaxed to sleep.

Mae and Claire chatted incessantly while they worked in the large back room of Mr. Shoemacher's shop, since their sewing machines were side by side. The other women paid them no mind because of the cacophony their own machines created. Besides, they were each involved in their own discussions about the men in their lives, their children, recipes, and the latest fashions.

Claire brushed aside a dangling brunette curl from her forehead and continued, "Then the bastard told me to get out and stay out! It was *my* room, and this reprobate was kicking *me* out!"

"Oh gosh, Claire. What did you do?" Mae continued peddling her machine.

"I threw his shoes at his head and told him, 'Look, schmuck, this is my room and I'm not going anywhere!'"

"That took a lot of courage. Weren't you afraid?" Mae snipped the thread, and placed the finished shirtwaist on the pile to her left.

"Nah! This wasn't the first time I had to deal with some fella giving me a hard time. I don't know why, but I always seem to pick from the bottom of the barrel." She lifted the presser foot and turned the fabric to reverse stitch the end of the seam. "Sometimes I think I oughta give up looking for another husband. After my first, you would think I'd know better."

"With your beauty, I can't imagine any man not wanting to marry you. You're the spit and image of an actress I saw once in a picture show ... can't remember her name." Mae grabbed the next piece of fabric and added, "But she had your coloring and figure."

"Now see? That's why you're my best friend. It's that sense of humor of yours!"

"Go on ... make jokes. But I'm serious, Claire. I know the look an actress must have. I've been studying it most of my life. That's why I came West from Philadelphia in the first place ... to be an actress on the stage."

"Gee whiz, Mae! You never told me that before. That explains why we got along right from the first day you walked into the shop. I don't talk about it much anymore, but I used to be a dancer in the chorus line at the Los Angeles Theater. You know the one, over on Spring Street, near Fourth."

"You did? How wonderful!"

"Of course, all that happened before Harry came along and saved me from a life of sin. I sure miss all the razzle-dazzle, though. Ah, those were the days." Claire cocked her head and looked starry-eyed above her sewing machine for a moment, before hunching over and peddling the treadle until her machine produced its familiar whir.

Mae's Revenge

"A dancer? That explains your svelte figure. So, we're both ladies of the theater at heart!" Mae chuckled to herself. *If you only knew how much acting I've done since we met ... you wouldn't believe it. Hope I never have to tell you, my friend.*

CHAPTER ELEVEN

I wonder where he could be ... must be at least eight o'clock—the sun went down a while ago. Mae shooed a fly away from the bowl of oranges on the square dark walnut table. She smiled as she toggled the switch on the electric floor lamp, straightened the fringed shade, and looked around her new home. She and Gus occupied one of three rented rooms on the second floor of a large Victorian near the center of town. They now had a wardrobe, next to their tall golden oak headboard, to store their clothes. They also had hot and cold running water to wash the dishes, their clothes, and themselves. But her favorite thing about their room was the large double-hung window by the sink. *Best thing I ever did was convince Gus to cough up some of that money he had stashed. Don't know what the hell he was saving it for.* She went to the window and brushed the lace curtain aside to look down on the wide street in front of the building. *No sign of him. Hmm.*

Mae's Revenge

They had left the rooming house three months earlier and moved into a respectable boardinghouse after Gus gained employment as a bank clerk. During one of his better moods, he took Mae to see the Pacific Ocean, at last. She squealed like a little girl as she ran into the waves, ignoring the salty sea spray soaking her clothes. Life was on a good path for the first time in a very long time.

But tonight he was late, and she began to worry. *Don't you go getting yourself killed, now that things are looking up!* Mulling over possible scenarios of his demise, she didn't hear him approach.

"Damn, Mae! It's hot as a whorehouse on nickel night!" Gus stumbled through the door and slumped onto a chair at the table. He propped his feet up on the seat of the opposite one.

"A whorehouse on nickel night? That's all you've got to say for yourself?"

"I guess I'm in the soup now, huh?" He gave her a cockeyed grin.

"You're damn right!" Mae knocked his feet off the seat of the other chair and sat down. "Gus, where have you been? I started to get the willies, imagining you beaten up and robbed, or God forbid, dead in some alleyway."

"Aw, Annie Mae, you know you don't have to worry about me. I can handle myself in a—"

"But now I see you were just on another bender!" Her head throbbed. She leaned her elbows on the table and tried rubbing her temples, but it was no use. Her heart ached, knowing he was returning to his old abusive ways. The memories of the beatings she'd endured came into focus. "You were doing so good staying away from the drink, Gus. What happened this time?"

"What happened *this time*? I'll tell you what happened!" He wiped his nose on his sleeve. "I was celebrating, Mae. I got a raise down at the bank today," he slurred. Now he began to yell. "Most women would be happy! But no ... not you. I never do anything good enough to suit you, Miss High and Mighty." He got up and began pacing around the room.

Mae began to speak, but Gus backhanded her before she managed to say anything. He struck her so hard the chair tilted and she fell to the floor.

"Gus, please! Don't do this again!" He was cowering over her now. His heavy breathing pressed down on her like a putrid shroud. She covered her face with both hands, cringing in anticipation of his next blow. But none came. Instead, he stepped back unsteadily, shook his head and slapped his hands to his sides, then staggered out the door—but not before punching a hole in the wall.

For the next few minutes, Mae lay there holding her jaw and sobbing. *I hope you get run over by a horse, you bastard! I can't take this anymore. I won't take this anymore.* As her anger grew she gathered herself up and went to the sink. She ran a dish rag under cold water and pressed it to her face. She stood in front of the mirror near the bed and removed the cloth to examine the damage. The swelling had already begun. She ran more cold water over the cloth, reapplied it to her face, and sat back down at the table. *Hope to God he doesn't come back tonight. If he does, I swear, I'll kill him.*

Mae's Revenge

Gus was still nowhere to be found when Mae left for work in the morning. She was glad. She looked up to discover a Mourning dove coo-cooing on a nearby rooftop. The soft, reassuring sound fit her mood. Friendly greetings from passersby were returned with a smile. Mae strode under the awning of the hardware store on Main Street. That's where a pyramid window display of brightly colored boxes, decorated with rats lying on their backs, feet stuck in the air, caught her eye. The labels read: "Rough on Rats ... kills rats, mice, flies, roaches, and bedbugs ... fifteen cents per box." Mae checked the store's hours, which were listed on a cardboard propped in the corner of the window. *Good. Open until six o'clock each evening.* A strange calm fell over her while she walked to the shop.

"Holy hell, Mae. What happened to you this time?" Claire asked when she arrived.

"It's nothing, really. I tripped going up the stairs to our room last night. In too much of a hurry to get home to Gus, I suppose." *Guess I'll always be an actress at heart.*

Claire took off her hat, grinned, and said, "No man could ever make *me* run home like that."

"I don't doubt that for a minute!" Mae attempted a smile, but the pain in her jaw restricted her reaction to a grimace.

"Last time, you said you tripped going *down* the stairs. Maybe from now on you should take the stairs sitting on your backside! But seriously, Mae, it doesn't look like nothing. It looks awful. Does it hurt?"

"A little, when I touch it. But it's honestly nothing to be concerned about, Claire. I'll be fine."

"If you say so. I sure hope that man of yours appreciates all you do for him."

"Don't be silly. Of course he does. I tell him all the time how lucky he is to have me!"

Claire chuckled and the two friends continued to work in silence, for a change, until the time to take a break for lunch came at noon.

They sat on the bench in front of the shop sharing the contents of the lunch pail Claire had brought from home. She tore a half of her ham sandwich off and handed it to Mae. "Here. You've got to eat something, and I need to lose a few pounds anyway."

"No, you don't. You're fine just the way you are." Mae took the food and said, "I was in such a rush to get to work on time I skipped making myself something." She took a bite. "This is delicious, thanks."

"You're welcome. Does it hurt to chew?"

"Stop worrying about me. I'm fine," Mae lied. She tried not to wince as she took another bite. "Claire, did you see the big sign in the window of the druggist? It said that old empty dance hall around the corner is up for sale."

Claire swallowed and then said, "Great. As soon as I get paid this week, I'll go buy it. Why the hell are you telling me about this, Mae?" She handed Mae her thermos. "Here, have some lemonade … I think you've got a fever!"

Mae accepted the offer and took a gulp before responding. A carriage horse decided at that moment to deposit a load of manure right in front of them. "Pee-yew! Let's get back to the shop," Mae said.

"I'm right behind you!"

Mae's Revenge

Mae opened the door and held it for Claire. "I was thinking, uh, maybe someday you and I might put our savings together and, uh, maybe start our own theater group."

"Gee, Mae ... are you sure you didn't crack your skull on those steps? I don't know about you, but it would take me about a hundred years to save enough to buy such a wonderful place ... or any place, for that matter!" She giggled and added, "Unless you want me to help you rob a bank or something!"

"Don't be dotty, Claire. I would never ask you to help me break the law ... I can do that all by myself!" Actress Mae threw her head back and laughed heartily, then palmed her aching jaw. "C'mon, silly, we better get back to work before we lose our jobs and then neither of us will have a penny to our name!"

As the afternoon wore on, Mae's jaw began to throb more, keeping their conversations to a minimum. Claire decided it her was duty to provide most of the banter to take her friend's mind off her discomfort.

"So, here's what I'm proposing, Mae. Next week is La Fiesta de Los Angeles, and I think we should go."

"I have no idea what that is."

"Oh, that's right; this is your first spring here. Well, it's this spectacular four-day event that happens every year. There's a huge parade on Broadway with floats and flowers everywhere, athletic competitions where we get to see all the men flex their muscles, and there's usually at least one ball. We wouldn't have to go to the ball because we couldn't afford proper gowns ... say, you don't happen to have a couple laying around at home, do you?"

Mae attempted a smile. "Don't be ridiculous."

Mr. Shoemacher interrupted by walking between them to go to the pattern table in the back to give instructions to the cutters. They stayed quiet until he passed back through the doorway to the front of the shop, where a customer was waiting.

"Anyway, as I was saying, we should try to at least go to the parade next Saturday. Mr. Shoemacher always closes the shop on parade day, because with all the festivities, there won't be any new customers coming in."

"Glad you told me."

"Yeah. And then we can go to Elysian Park to watch the competitions. Maybe I'll find my next husband out there."

"I'll think about it. I'll ask Gus tonight." *If he's sober.*

"C'mon, Mae. A girl's gotta have some fun in this life." Claire folded the shirt she had been working on. "There, that's the last for today." She stood, put on her hat, and added, "You'd better go home and put a cold cloth on that face of yours before Gus gets home. You don't want him to see you looking like a retired prizefighter."

"You're probably right."

Mae, Claire, and the other women cleaned up their work areas and paraded out of the shop, after each, in turn, said good night to Mr. Shoemacher.

Gus wasn't there when Mae arrived home. She immediately placed a cool wet rag on her face and took a seat at the table. Sitting there, absentmindedly looking around the room, she noticed the end of one of the floorboards by Gus's side of the bed sticking up ever so slightly. *Must be the angle of the sunset creating a shadow.*

Curious now, Mae put the rag down and went over to the bed. She got down on her hands and knees and saw the floorboard was indeed out of alignment. She tapped the end of the board in question with the heel of her hand and discovered all nails meant to hold it in place were missing. *That's strange. I never noticed this before.*

Mae pried the board out of its allotted space and gasped. *What the hell have you been doing, Gus?* She reached into the shadowy opening and pulled out three large stacks of bills tied neatly with string. *There must be hundreds of dollars here!* Her heartbeat pounded against her eardrums so hard she glanced behind to see if anyone else heard the racket. *Nobody. Thank God.* Mae's stomach ached. Her nerves couldn't take any more, so she quickly returned the stacks of cash to their hiding place and moved the board back into its slot, careful to leave the same end slightly ajar.

Just as she took her seat back at the table and raised the cool cloth to her jaw, Gus came through the door.

"How was your day?" Mae said. Her hand trembled as she moved the cloth higher on her face.

"Sorry about the other night. Let me see your face," he responded.

Mae moved the cloth away and lifted her chin so Gus could take a good look.

Gus bent down to get a closer view of the damage he'd inflicted. "Shit. Sorry. You just make me go crazy sometimes, ya know? Especially when I've had a few." He hung his hat on the hook next to the door and sat opposite her. He looked over his shoulder at the bottle of whiskey on the shelf above the sink. "I sure could use a drink. But I guess I better not, huh?"

Mae glared at him.

"Okay. Okay. I get it. I said I'm sorry. Can we just forget it?"

Mae stayed silent.

Gus continued, "So how about me getting a raise? That's good news. Right?"

Hmpf! A raise. I'll bet. Probably been stealing from the bank since the day you started working there.

Mae studied his face, looking for any sign of the man she'd fallen in love with so many years ago. There was none.

"Yes, a raise is very good news. Speaking of money, may I have three dollars?"

"What the hell for?"

"Claire invited me to go with her to the annual parade and carnival next week, and I'll need some money for a new pair of shoes. The ones I have will never do for a full day of walking around town. The soles are worn clear through." Mae held up her right foot. "See?"

"Damn. You weren't kidding. Sure. I'll give it to you tomorrow."

"Can't you give it to me tonight? Then I can shop on my way home from work tomorrow."

"Uh, no. I have to, uh, get it from my account at the bank. I'll get it for you tomorrow." Gus looked over at the whiskey again.

Mae enjoyed watching him squirm. *I'll get it myself after you leave in the morning.*

CHAPTER TWELVE

"Sit down!" Gus shoved Mae onto the chair. "You're not going anywhere near that parade tomorrow." Gus belched, and then continued his rant. "I know what you and that bitch, Claire, are up to. You think you're gonna make serious money by screwing some big-shot political types who always show up at those things."

"She's not a bitch. She's my friend. You can't stand it because you don't have any friends!" Mae tried to back away from Gus, but her hip bumped into the corner of the table. Her eyes clenched shut for a moment as she winced … just long enough for Gus to reach her and place his hands around her neck.

Mae could not believe her husband would seriously try to kill her. Her eyes opened wide as she stared into his hate-filled expression. "Oh Gus—for God's sake—what are you doing?" She clawed at his wrists, trying to get him to release her.

His grip on her throat tightened. "No other man is ever going to have you," he slurred. "I'll kill you before I let that happen!"

Mae gasped for air as she reached behind and felt for the whiskey bottle on the table. As he squeezed tighter, she swung the bottle. The blood spray created as the bottle broke on Gus's forehead splattered her face, too. When Gus released his grip to wipe the blood from his eyes, Mae ducked away from him and ran out of their room and down the steps, wiping her face on her apron as she ran.

Mae rested on a bench around the corner to catch her breath, then walked for hours before daring to return home. Eventually, she stood across the street from the old Victorian and saw there was no light illuminating their window. She decided Gus must have left or had passed out. She hoped he was gone. He was. Mae slid the bolt on the lock and went to bed.

Mae awoke late the next morning. Her throat still hurt and she was not in the mood to rush to a parade. Claire was glad to meet Mae at the edge of Elysian Park after the parade. She refrained from quizzing her friend about the reason she missed the parade that morning.

Mae hoped Claire would accept her explanation. "Claire, I'm so sorry. When I woke up this morning, my stomach was so upset I thought I might not be able to join you at all today." She fingered her stiff lace collar choking her bruised neck.

"Are you sure you're up to watching the athletic competitions?"

"Yes. Yes, I'm feeling much better now. Look, I've even got new shoes for the occasion!" Mae stuck her left foot out from beneath her long skirt.

Claire glanced down and then at her friend's pale face. "Mae, are you sure you're alright?

"Of course. Now, we'd better get a move on, or you'll

Mae's Revenge

miss your chance to pick a new husband!" She forced a smile.

The friends selected a bench under a broad-leafed tree to avoid getting sunburned. Two barrel-chested men were locked in various wrestling holds on a mat in the clearing before them. Claire studied the combatants closely. Mae brooded, recalling the previous night.

Gus was there when she returned home Saturday evening. There was no discussion between them. Mae clung to her side of the bed through the night. Their silence continued through the next day, except for the occasional necessary communication through supper, such as "pass the potatoes."

The following Monday, Mae stopped by the hardware store in the early evening after work. It was the gray time of day when everything beyond a few feet appeared to be a silhouette. She heard the coo-cooing of the Mourning dove once again, but only saw its outline on the roof before it flew away. After making her purchase, she continued her walk home mulling over the situation. *All my life I've had men telling me to do this or do that, or else. No more! But who would have ever thought, now that I'm on my own, this would be my first independent decision?* Mae shook off the sudden chill gripping her spine and hastened her step.

"So? You finally decided to come home, I see," Gus groused. "Where the hell have you been?" He did not get up from the table to greet Mae. He must have skipped work again, because he normally would not have gotten home before her.

"I could ask you the same thing. Where were you all night?" Mae put the box under the sink, then removed her hat and hung it on the wooden coat tree by the door.

"And what's that you've got there?" Gus asked, ignoring her question.

"Oh, that? It's nothing. Something I picked up to get rid of the mice in the shop. Mr. Shoemacher asked me to buy it on my way home."

"So now we're paying to get rid of rats for Mr. Shoemacher, are we? Does that bastard think we're flush from the pittance he pays you?" Gus pushed his chair back from the table. "Or do you two have something going on behind my back?" He tried to stand, but stumbled instead.

"Sit down! Don't be ridiculous! You're drunk. He's an old man. He said he would pay me back tomorrow."

Gus regained his seat and took another swallow from the half-empty brown bottle of whiskey. "What else does he have to pay you back for, I wonder?" Gus sneered at her.

Mae looked away, determined not to be dragged into another argument. Not tonight. "Are you hungry?" she called over her shoulder as she put the cast iron pot on the stove. "You probably haven't eaten, have you? I'm going to make some soup with the potatoes and carrots I've still got in the bin." She began cutting up the vegetables and throwing them in the pot with some water and salt and pepper.

Gus didn't respond. He had fallen asleep sitting with his crossed arms propping him up at the table. His head bowed onto his chest as he snored and snorted.

Mae's Revenge

Good. You sleep. Now, should I put it in the whiskey or the soup? Soup. God knows he'll notice if his drink tastes different. I wonder how much it will take? I should have asked at the hardware store how much to use to kill a large rat. She looked over at the sleeping drunk. *Maybe it says on the box.* Mae got the box from under the sink and read the instructions. She shook some of its contents into the soup pot. *That doesn't seem like enough. Better give it a couple more shakes. There, that should do it.* She looked at the ceiling and said to herself, "God forgive me."

Gus woke with a start, swiped the drool from the side of his mouth with the back of his hand, and wiped it on his pant leg. "Something smells good. Is that soup ready yet? I'm starved. I could eat the whole pot."

"Yes, it's ready. And I don't care if you do eat it all. I'm not very hungry. It's my time of the month and these cramps have got the best of me. Here." She handed him a large bowlful of the piping hot soup and a spoon.

Mae sat opposite him at the table, watching him closely, in nervous anticipation.

The bowl is almost empty. How can he still be gobbling it up? Oh my God—what if I didn't use enough?

She had no sooner finished that thought than Gus abruptly fell sideways and cracked his skull when he hit the floor. His eyes rolled back in his head as he gagged and gurgled, and then he made no sound at all. A pool of blood spread around where his head lolled to the side.

Frozen, Mae did not get up from her chair to check on him. After what seemed like hours, she cleared the table and washed the bowl and spoon. She left the open whiskey bottle still sitting at his place at the table. She poured the remainder of the soup into a bucket, tossed the poison box in, and shoved it under the bed for now, which allowed her to wash the soup pot too. She'd worry about what to do with the bucket later. All the while, she dared not look at her murdered husband splayed out on the floor.

Now what? Mae suddenly realized she hadn't thought the whole thing through. The killing was done, true enough. But how could she get rid of his body and explain Gus's death?

Several hours passed before she had a plan.

Carefully, Mae pulled his watch out of his pocket and saw it was well past midnight. She lifted Gus's bloody head and wrapped it in the small throw rug from the foot of their bed. Grabbing him under the arms, she strained every muscle pulling and dragging him over to the door.

Mae scrubbed the floor where, by now, Gus's blood had created a dark coagulated puddle. She washed the bucket, brush, and her hands to remove any evidence. Satisfied no one would notice the spot, she opened the door and looked down the hall to make sure all was quiet. The other two boarders' rooms on that floor were across from each other, at the far end of the hall, separated from theirs by a storage room and a large broom closet. Fortunately, the stairway emanated from their end of the hall, right outside their room. It took all her strength to pull him around the corner and give his body one strong shove. She almost forgot to grab the bloody rug, but managed to grip a corner before Gus's body made its last trip down the stairs. Frightened by the terrible noise he made as he tumbled down, arms and legs flailing like a rag doll, Mae retreated to their room, quickly closed the door, and threw the bloody

Mae's Revenge

rug under the bed. She leaned her back against the door and stood there panting, listening for any response in the hallway. There was none. She let out a quick gasp when she saw the brown bottle still sitting on the table.

Mae quickly grabbed the whiskey bottle, returned to the top of the stairs, and tossed it down on top of her dead husband. Only then, did she begin to scream for help.

She told her story over and over again. She told everyone about the shock of seeing her poor Gus at the bottom of the steps with blood streaks covering his handsome face. About how she rushed down the stairs to see if he was still alive. She did rush down the steps, but it was to be seen cradling her dead husband when the first witness arrived. "That's how I got this blood all over me. Must have been drinking again and lost his balance. I was worried, you see, and stayed up waiting for him. When all of a sudden I heard an awful rumbling sound, I rushed out, but I got to him too late." She began to cry again. "My husband, my love, was just lying there dead."

Mae's acting talent served her well as she wailed hysterically while the woman who ran the boardinghouse attempted to console her.

At last the undertaker removed Gus's remains.

Everyone expressed their condolences before returning to their own beds.

It was almost dawn. Mae was spent. She knew she would be expected at work in a couple of hours. Work would be impossible today. She'd go to the shop and explain to Mr. Shoemacher about Gus's untimely death.

He wouldn't want her to stay at the shop considering the circumstances.

Mae flopped across the bed without pulling down the coverlet. When sleep started to come, she told herself *... I'll just nap a bit. Then I'll go tell him. And Claire. I have to tell Claire. The truth? We'll see ... I dunno ... maybe.*

CHAPTER THIRTEEN

Other than the women she worked with, Mr. Shoemacher, and a couple of Gus's drinking friends from the bank, there were no other mourners. Mae felt all their eyes following her every reaction until, at last, the preacher scooped up a handful of dirt and let it funnel through the breeze back to the earth with the familiar "ashes to ashes" pronouncement. For good measure, she forced one last lone tear to cascade over her cheek. The other attendees took her hand in turn and, with sincere concern in their voices, offered condolences before dispersing.

Mae and Claire walked slowly, arm-in-arm, down the dirt path leading out of the cemetery.

Mae was silent. In truth, she was deep in thought, going over her plans for the future. *I hope it's still for sale. I wonder how much they want for it?*

Claire startled her back to the present by leaning in and whispering, "You're not upset that he's dead, are you?"

"Don't be ridiculous! Of course I'm upset."

"Mae, you can tell me. I've seen all the bruises and scrapes when you've come limping into work. Nobody trips that much. He was beating you, wasn't he?"

Mae stopped midstride and began to cry real tears. "I'm so ashamed." She covered her face with both hands. The confession gushed out of her like water from a clogged faucet, in fits and spurts. "It started back in Iowa ... hoped it would be better in California ... not able to have kids ... horrible temper ... stole money ... drunk most of the time ... couldn't take it anymore."

Claire tried not to react as she took it all in. When, at last, Mae finished, she held out her handkerchief. "Here, use this—you're full of snot, you look a mess!" She chuckled nervously.

"I'm full of snot? That's all you've got to say after everything I've told you?" Mae looked at her friend in disbelief as she took the hanky and began wiping her face. And then, she too, started to chuckle.

"He got what he deserved," Claire said. "Bastard ... they should all get what they deserve!"

"Oh my God, Claire. I did it. I'm finally free for the first time in my life, with no man to tell me what to do anymore! But you've got to swear to not tell a soul!"

Indignant, Claire said, "*I* won't tell anyone."

"Swear it!"

"I swear on Harry's grave I won't tell a soul!"

"Harry's grave?"

"Yeah, well, uh ... that's a story for another day." Claire took her arm and started down the path again. "C'mon, Mae. It's been a very trying day, and we've got to get you home."

CHAPTER FOURTEEN

Mae was amazed at how much money had been hidden under the floorboards. The first thing she did the day after the funeral was deposit it in the bank. Not the bank where Gus worked—she didn't dare risk that. *If they suspected him, they would have come after it by now, wouldn't they? Besides ... after all he put me through, I deserve some compensation. He certainly didn't have any bonds or life insurance for me to live on.*

At the shop later that day, Mae overheard one of the other women, Lizzy, discussing a meeting she planned to attend that evening; something to do with putting on a stage show to raise money for the orphans of San Gabriel.

Mae called to her over the din of the Singer machines, "Where is the meeting you're talking about? I'd love to join you. I mean, we'd love to join you—wouldn't we, Claire?"

Claire looked at Mae for a moment before looking over her shoulder and responding, "Yeah, Lizzy, we'd love to!" Looking back at Mae, she mouthed, "We would?" Mae nodded.

"Of course you can come," Lizzy said. "You can both come. We need all the help we can get. We're meeting at six thirty at my friend Naomi's place. You two can walk over there with me after work, if you want."

In unison, Mae and Claire said, "Thanks!"

Eight women, including Mae and Claire, attended the planning meeting after work: Naomi, Lizzy, Franny, Matilda (everyone called her Tilly), Kate, and Samantha. Mae quickly determined not a one of them had any theatrical experience—except Claire, of course.

Emboldened by her newfound freedom, Mae began to take control almost immediately, offering to write down any ideas they came up with. The ladies decided they would perform a couple of duets (Naomi and Samantha apparently had fair voices, according to the others) and perhaps Franny, Matilda, and Kate could join Claire for a dance number, if she'd be willing to teach them the steps. "Sure, I will," Claire agreed. "If I can remember them myself. It's been a while." That left Lizzy and Mae.

"Well, I can't sing or dance for the life of me, but I can play the piano!" Lizzy announced. "I haven't really practiced since Teddy left me, but I'm sure I'm still able to plunk out a tune or two."

"That's wonderful," Mae said. "And I would gladly do a dramatic reading. Perhaps something from Arthur Conan Doyle's *The Adventures of Sherlock Holmes?*"

Mae's Revenge

Everyone expressed their excitement about the progress they were making, until Mae asked the most important question of the evening: where would they perform?

Their enthusiasm evaporated.

"I need a drink," Naomi said and got up from the table to take down a bottle of whiskey from the shelf above her scrub-worn porcelain kitchen sink. "Me too," the others chimed in.

"Fear not, ladies! Give us a little time to consider it," Mae said. "We'll come up with something—won't we, Claire?"

"We will? I mean, of course we will! Don't worry, by the time we have our next meeting it will be all settled. Right, Mae?"

CHAPTER FIFTEEN

Claire waited on the corner, where she stood wilting in the blistering heat for what seemed like hours. Her curls were damp and starting to frizz. She knew she must look a sight. She tried to casually wipe the perspiration from her upper lip when an attractive gentleman, a bit her junior, tipped his hat to her as he passed. Claire cocked her head as he walked away. Was that a smile, or a sneer?

At last, she saw Mae approaching. "So, what did he say? How much is the sale price? Can we, I mean you, afford it? When can we tell the other girls?"

"Hold your horses. One question at a time." Mae was out of breath from scurrying to tell her friend the news.

"But did you get it? I should have gone with you … I'm much better with figures than you. I hope you didn't agree to the first number that blowhard threw out. You should have let me do the negotiating." She hesitated, then said, "We didn't get it, did we?"

Mae started to laugh. "Will you calm down? Did you really expect I would let that old windbag bilk me out of money I did murder for? Don't be a pinhead, Claire. Of course, we got it. We can start clearing it out and setting up the stage next week."

Claire grabbed her and hugged her hard. "Annie Mae Steinberg Milmott, I love you!" Two well-dressed older gentlemen passed by at that moment, harrumphed, and gave them a disapproving glare.

Mae pushed her away and laughed. "You can drop the Milmott part from now on."

"Ooh, Mae, you're so naughty!"

"I don't feel naughty ... I feel liberated. So, what do you think? Should we have a meeting with the others to decide on a name, or shall the two of us decide by ourselves?"

"I think you should get to decide, since it was your idea and your money ... well, Gus's money."

"But he's not here now, is he?" Mae took pleasure in saying that, and gave her friend a mischievous grin. "I've been thinking maybe something exotic."

"How about French?"

"Since when," Mae asked, "do you know French?"

"Remember when I used to see that tall, good-looking fellow from Montreal with the gold pocket watch? I know, I know. He turned out to be another cad, but he *did* teach me a few words in French ... How about, Mari Mort Theater?"

"Ooh ... I like the sound of that, but what does it mean?"

Claire linked Mae's arm as they walked down the avenue, leaned in close, and whispered.

Mae stopped abruptly, looked at her friend's glistening face, and then they both burst into laughter.

Finale!

EPILOGUE

November 19, 1900

Dear Papa,

Wonderful news!

Tell Mama that I, along with my best friend, Claire (I wrote you about her before), and some of the other talented women I've met, have opened our very own theater! I was able to buy the building with the money poor Gus left me. We worked our fingers to the bone cleaning and remodeling the interior of an old, abandoned dance hall and now it is ~~beutiful~~ beautiful—if I do say so myself!

We did our first performance as a charity show for orphans, but after that we started charging seventy-five cents per person. It's been a huge success, and by this time next year I should be able to come home and spend Chanukah and Christmas in ~~Phildelphia~~ Philadelphia with you, Mama, and the rest of the family—at long last!

Sorry this letter is so short, but I've got to get to rehearsal. (Notice, I have also learned to typewrite. I'm using our stage manager's Remington to type this, and she's waiting anxiously for me to finish.)

I pray you are all well.

Have the Happiest Chanukah and the Merriest Christmas ever. I hope you get lots of snow!

Your devoted daughter,

Annie Mae

Acknowledgements

First, and foremost, I must thank Kay Murray, who I was fortunate to meet through Ancestry.com. Kay provided the information regarding Mae's ability to paint, and sent me a digital copy of a framed oil painting of pink roses handed down to her son. In addition, and most importantly, the photograph of the real Mae used on the book cover was also generously provided by Kay, along with her permission to reproduce it for this book. I cannot tell you what a thrill it was to be looking into the eyes of my great-aunt for the first time.

Next, I am happy to thank my husband and fellow author, Michael R. Stern, for his continuing support through this adventure. (His Quantum Touch time-travel series can be found on Amazon.)

Lourdes Venard, of Comma Sense Editing, once again guided this project seamlessly through to completion, and I thank her most sincerely.

Cover production artist and interior layout master Jack and Elizabeth Parry have once again proved there is a reason they are called professionals.

A special note of thanks must go to you, dear reader, for taking time from your busy life to spend a bit of it with the imaginary world I have created here. For that, I am truly grateful.

If you have enjoyed: *Mae's Revenge*—

Pencil in: *Standing Ovation*—**Second Act of the "Mari Mort Theater" trilogy.**

About the Author

L.C. Bennett Stern was born in Philadelphia, but was raised from a young age in southern New Jersey, as the middle child in a family of nine. She is a member of the Historical Novel Society, as well as Philadelphia Hometown Reads, #The Awethors, South Jersey Women for Progressive Change, and Birds of the Eastern United States, online sites.

Her first book, ***Bosses and Blackjacks: A Tale of the "Bloody Fifth" in Philadelphia***, tells the true story of her paternal grandfather, David Bennett, a police lieutenant who becomes embroiled in a political scandal with the mayor and a butcher, resulting in a murder on Election Day in 1917. The trial that ensues is national news, sharing headlines with WWI.

Mae's Revenge is a fictionalized tale, built upon some basic truths, about one of David's older sisters.

Linda is the mother of two grown children, a daughter and a son, and lives with her husband and their adorable Wheaton Terrier, Katie Scarlett, in a small river town directly across the Delaware from Philadelphia.

Facebook:	L.C. Bennett Stern
Twitter:	@lcbennettstern
Website:	www.lcbennettstern.com
Email:	lcstern21@gmail.com

> Why authors want Amazon reviews
>
> If a book gets 10 reviews the author receives a cryptic fragment of a treasure map.
>
> If a book gets 30 reviews the Bank of England will then accept copies of the book as legal tender.
>
> If a book gets 50 reviews Amazon sends the author a free unicorn.
>
> Why not help an author you love get a free unicorn by reviewing their book today!

Please help L.C. Bennett Stern get a unicorn.

She promises to take very good care of it!